She was hung up on her ex. Did he want to get mixed up in that?

Sandro walked over to the bar and set their glasses in the sink. On the other hand, what did it matter to him? In a few days, none of this would matter.

"Are you offering your...services?" she asked.

He leaned close. This time he kissed the corner of her mouth. "When you put it like that, it sounds as dirty as it should be."

She went perfectly still. He breathed in her sweet floral perfume and he had his answer. He wanted to get mixed up in whatever this was.

"I wouldn't say no," she said.

That was a start. "I need you to say yes."

She took one step closer and whispered her answer. "Yes."

* * *

What Happens in Miami... by Nadine Gonzalez is part of the Miami Famous series.

Dear Reader,

Every December, Art Basel draws an eclectic crowd to Miami Beach for a celebration of modern art. Known for over-the-top exhibits and outlandish parties, Art Basel is a carnival of delights. Why, though, does acclaimed actor Alessandro Cardenas want to hop off the carousel the moment he meets Angeline Louis? Read and find out!

What Happens in Miami... is the second stand-alone novel of the Miami Famous series, which taps into the city's natural diversity to spin modern-day love stories. *Scandal in the VIP Suite* kicks off the series with the unforgettable story of Julian and Nina.

For more about my upcoming releases, visit www.nadine-gonzalez.com and follow on Instagram and Twitter, @_nadinegonzalez. Need more Miami modern love? Check out the Miami Dreams series with Harlequin Kimani.

I hope you fall hard for Angel and Sandro!

Nadine

NADINE GONZALEZ

WHAT HAPPENS IN MIAMI...

Recycling programs
for this product may
not exist in your area.

ISBN-13: 978-1-335-23298-4

What Happens in Miami...

Harlequin Enterprises ULC
22 Adelaide St. West, 40th Floor
Toronto, Ontario M5H 4E3, Canada
www.Harlequin.com

Printed in U.S.A.

Nadine Gonzalez is an attorney and a romance novelist. *Kirkus Reviews* has described her work as "sleek and entertaining...[with] vibrant settings, appealing characters, and a sexy and nuanced love story."

Nadine lives in Miami with her husband and their son.

For more information visit her website, nadine-gonzalez.com.

Books by Nadine Gonzalez

Harlequin Desire

Miami Famous

Scandal in the VIP Suite
What Happens in Miami...

Harlequin Kimani Romance

Exclusively Yours
Unconditionally Mine

Visit her Author Profile page at Harlequin.com, or nadine-gonzalez.com, for more titles.

You can also find Nadine Gonzalez on Facebook, along with other Harlequin Desire authors, at Facebook.com/harlequindesireauthors.

To my editor, Errin Toma, thanks for coaxing the best possible story out of me. There would be no Miami Famous series without your vision. I am looking forward to our future projects.

Special thanks to my agent, Jessica Alvarez. I am thrilled to join your team.

To my sister, Martine, thanks for your friendship and your love. To my lively family, particularly those on the group chat, thanks for sharing the highs and the lows.

As always, this novel is dedicated to Ariel and Nathaniel. Without your love, none of this matters.

BASELICIOUS

The prodigal son returns! Alessandro Cardenas ("Sandro" for his stans) was spotted at MIA late last night. The Academy Award winner and avid art collector is back in the Magic City for Art Basel Miami Beach. The weekend-long affair is a mix of glamour, culture and drunken good times that can only happen in Miami. Get ready! A-list celebrities will descend on our city to feast like royalty and party like beasts. Unlike the others, however, Cardenas may actually give a damn about art. The actor will donate a painting from his private collection to raise funds for Caribbean islands devastated by last summer's hurricanes. The international art fair starts tomorrow evening with a star-studded, invitation-only event. The rest of us will have to pay full price. Hopefully, we won't have to wait too long for another Cardenas sighting. We expect to run into the hottie at his favorite after-hours club, TENTEN, sometime between 4–6 a.m. #SandroFever

—@Sunshine&Wine_IG

One

Angel wasn't in the habit of taking impromptu mid-week boat rides, not anymore anyway, unless there was the promise of a major payoff, like a free night's stay on Grand Bahamas Island. And yet here she was on a Wednesday evening, on the deck of a speedboat, slicing through the bay, hair, scarf and the skirt of her dress flapping in the wind as sunset poured out its colors.

She was on her way to Fisher Island, a private residential enclave for the ridiculously rich. The barrier island off the coast of Miami Beach was accessible only by boat or aircraft. Anything the select few residents could ever want or need was ferried or flown in. For the residents, this was part of the appeal. For the random mainlander dispatched at the end of a long workday to deliver goods and services, it was an inconvenience, a pain, an encroachment on personal time, a—

Ouch!

The boat skipped on the choppy waves, tossing Angel on her side. The helmsman shouted for her to take a seat. She sat on the banquette and gripped the rail. You're lucky to be here, she reminded herself. This "plum" assignment had fallen on her lap due to a series of unfortunate events. Earlier today, Justine Carr, the art gallery's sales director, was dashing across Lincoln Road for a quick cup of coffee when a Mini Cooper hit her. Her injuries were not life threatening: a broken ankle and a bruised ego. The ensuing turmoil, however, was like nothing Angel had ever seen. It was Art Basel week, all-hands-on-deck week, no-time-to-mess-around-and-get-run-over-by-a-car week. After some quick reassignments, Angel, the newest member of Gallery Six, was tasked with picking up some of the slack.

The boat slowed and pulled up to a marina crowded with various yachts and the like. A man rushed forward to assist her. Angel handed him her metal briefcase instead. Then she slipped off her Louboutin mules and leaped off the boat unassisted. She was, after all, a lifelong Floridian.

A golf cart ride later, Angel arrived at Villa Paraiso, a bay-front compound that could have been copy/pasted from the hills of Capri. They drove through the gates and along a palm tree–lined path. After a brief interaction with the property's chief of security, she was allowed entrance into the main building. An elevator took her up to the penthouse on the tenth floor.

A housekeeper greeted her at the door, asked for her name and led her into a large living room. "Please wait here," she said.

Catching her breath, Angel took in the panoramic views of the bay she had just crossed and the skyline of the city she had left behind, all of it spread out under an orange-vanilla swirl sky.

Paradise, she mused. Only a quick jaunt across the bay. Who knew?

She placed the case with the painting on a console table and checked her appearance in the mirror hanging above it. She was a disheveled mess. The midi-length linen dress was wrinkled. Her hair… *Oh, God, my hair!* As she raked her fingers through her tangled chestnut-colored waves, she was forced to admit the boat ride had done some good. She was radiant! Her tawny brown skin glowed and her light eyes shone clear and bright. Fresh air was a hell of a boon.

She ought to get out more often.

There was plenty she ought to be doing more often: dating, sexting, socializing, jogging, maybe even scuba diving. All this focus on her career wasn't healthy. After, she promised herself. After…

Music, laughter and the smell of something delicious drifted in from somewhere. Was the client hosting a party? If he were, she wished he'd hurry up. The sooner they wrapped up this deal, the sooner she could get back to her life. So what if it involved eating crackers out of the box while waiting for the next installment of *My Ex Is Getting Along Just Fine Without Me* to upload on YouTube? That was her business.

She had expected a quick, discrete exchange in a home office setting. To her understanding, this was the standard practice with most collectors. Then again, this client was anything but standard.

To Angel's supreme irritation, her heartbeat ticked up with anticipation. Meeting with a buyer, no matter how rich, handsome and famous, should not provoke a flurry of butterflies. What next? Was she going to ask the man for an autograph? She was not going to make it in this business with that mindset. This was her new career path.

Dealing with the rich and famous was part of her job now. She could not afford to fail.

Last Tax Day, after her ex had moved out, Angel had come to the conclusion that her lifestyle could not be sustained on a starving artist's income. She had to face facts: her dream was dead and the time to mourn had passed. But if she could not sell her own art, what was stopping her from selling the work of other artists? Within weeks she'd landed a job at a prestigious Miami Beach gallery and earned enough to save up for Phase 2 of her plan. She wouldn't earn a commission on tonight's transaction, but she'd earn bonus points with her boss if she concluded the sale.

Angel checked her phone for the time. Only five minutes had passed. She had to chill out—famous people kept regular people waiting all the time.

Her trained eye zeroed in on the artwork. The space was, at its core, a gallery showcasing the homeowner's eclectic pieces, all periods and trends colliding. She went over to a pair of framed paintings on a far wall. One was of a red apple hanging from a tree branch. The other was of a woman sleeping in a garden. She was naked if you looked past the strategically placed fig leaf. Angel was trying to decipher the artist's signature when she heard the blunt sound of bare feet on tile. She glanced over her shoulder.

There he was, standing motionless by the sliding glass doors that opened onto a terrace. Whatever remained of the day's sunlight spilled onto his broad, bare shoulders. He was practically naked—if you looked past the damp swim trunks, which wasn't hard to do.

Tight and trim, he had the body of a lifelong swimmer. And it seemed to Angel that he had just emerged from the sea. His chest and limbs, sculpted and defined, glistened with water. His wavy black hair, cut close to the scalp, glistened. His bronze skin, touched by sunlight, glistened. With all that glistening sparkle, it was disquieting to meet his blank expression. His handsome face was impassive. From brow line to jawline, broad nose to full mouth, he gave nothing away. Was he perplexed to find her here? He'd been expecting Justine. Had anyone warned him?

But a sheepish grin quelled her fears.

"Sorry, I was expecting…" He paused to slip on a rumpled white shirt. "They said your name was Ángel and I figured…"

He figured she was a man. Common mistake. She'd gone to school with at least three guys named Ángel. To set the record straight, she stepped forward and introduced herself properly, business card and all. "Angeline Louis, sales associate with Gallery Six," she said. "Angel, for short."

He took the card and ran his thumb over the gallery's embossed logo. Under his breath, he repeated her name. "Angel." Why that moved her, she couldn't say. Then he introduced himself. "Alessandro Cardenas."

She would have liked to say: I know who you are. But that wasn't technically true. She knew his name, age and ethnicity: Alessandro D. Cardenas, thirty-two, Cuban American. She'd seen most of his movies, including *Shadows Need Light*, the indie film for which he'd won an Independent Spirit Award, a Golden Globe, and an Oscar for best supporting actor. She was familiar with the brands he promoted, his political leanings, and she could name a few of his famous exes. He was a sex symbol, a social media star and a darling of the critics, in that order. And, it seemed, he was a serious art collector. That was a lot to know about someone you'd never met. More than she knew about her next-door neighbor.

"A pleasure to meet you, Mr. Cardenas."

"Don't," he said. "Sandro...for short. Never Alé. When I was a kid, I had a cat by that name. She strayed, but she'll always be the one."

That didn't sound right. "A kid named Alessandro had a cat named Alé?"

"Short for Alley Cat. But I was ten, and a little narcissist."

"What's changed since you were ten?" Angel asked. She doubted that he'd grown out of his narcissistic tendencies.

He dropped her card on a low marble coffee table. "For one thing, I'm not little anymore."

Amen to that!

Despite her best efforts, her gaze swept down the length of his sculpted body. It was a shame that he'd covered up on her account. His shirt was as rumpled as her dress. However, the white cotton beautifully highlighted the sun-kissed patina of his skin.

Okay! Stop!

Not five minutes ago, she'd been nervous to meet him. Now they were chatting freely as if hanging out at a poolside bar. There must be a happy medium where she was more polished and professional, and he less naked and wet.

Angel took a moment to stitch her frayed wits together. But he wasted no time snipping the thread. He looked her dead in the eye. "*Temptation*."

"I'm sorry. What?" Had she wandered onto the set of a nineties Calvin Klein ad?

"The diptych." He pointed to the paintings that she'd been studying. "The first is Eve in her garden, the second is the apple hanging out of reach."

"Temptation," she repeated.

You didn't need a degree in biblical studies to catch the symbolism, but a few functioning brain cells would help. She should wrap this up before she made a fool of herself.

She went to the console table and retrieved the metal case. "As you requested, I have here—"

"Have you eaten?"

"Excuse me?"

"We just came back from the pool and were about to have dinner. Would you like to join us?"

Just the mention of dinner provoked a rumble in her tummy. Whatever was on the grill smelled divine. Even so, she had a job to do. That meant no ogling the client, no chitchatting with him and definitely no joining his friends for dinner. Those were the rules. Right?

"Sorry. I have a boat to catch."

"We can take you back at any time—unless you need to get home. In that case, I won't keep you."

Tomorrow was Art Basel's grand opening. The day promised to be long and grueling. She had to help with the final touches on the gallery's viewing room in advance of the star-studded VIP event. Angel had intended to spend the rest of her night accessorizing the outfit she'd selected. Then she was going to repeat the process with a backup outfit.

"I shouldn't," she said.

"Oh, you should," he said. "The chef from *Diablo* is at the grill recreating his bar menu classics. You won't want to miss out."

The metal handle of the case with the painting almost slipped from her hand. Had she heard him correctly? Myles V. Paquin, known as MVP, was a Miami culinary sensation and a master of fusion cuisine. His restaurant in the Design District, *Diablo*, was a hot spot. It wasn't Michelin star-rated or anything, but it was *the* place for brunch and dinner. She had wanted to celebrate her thirtieth birthday at the restaurant this year but no luck. Not one seat was available.

"You came all this way," he said. "At least let me feed you."

Angel swallowed the last bits of her resolve. Not only was she staying for dinner, if he kept this up, she might eat out of his hands.

Two

Angel was in paradise.

Chef MVP fussed over kebabs on a massive grill. Grammy winner DJ Jordan regaled the table with tales of drunken nights in Ibiza. Fashion models Jenny Xi and Rose Rachid, an exceptionally attractive couple, shared recipes and real estate investment tips. Alessandro (she refused to call him Sandro) played the role of the solicitous host. He was the life pulse of the party, readily sampling Myles's spicy grilled corn, laughing at Jordan's corny jokes, and asking Rose follow-up questions. At some point he passed Jenny the name and number of his real estate agent. As he juggled those tasks, he kept Angel's wineglass full and encouraged her to sample every dish. All of this took place on a terrace that stretched out beneath the stars.

During dessert, he pulled up a chair next to hers. His bathing suit was dry and the buttons of his shirt had been left undone. Relaxed and happy, he looked centerfold ready.

"Do you like working for Gallery Six?" he asked.

He was probably just making conversation, but he'd hit a sore spot. Gallery Six was one of South Florida's premier galleries, one of only two that had been invited to show at Art Basel. Truthfully, it was a bit pretentious for Angel's tastes, but she wouldn't complain. Not everyone got to follow their life's true calling or succeed at the career of their choice. "It's an exciting place to work," she said. That wasn't too far from the truth.

"Have you worked there long?"

"Under a year." Angel took a sip of wine. Their conversation was getting lopsided. She ought to reciprocate, show some interest in his work. "I liked you in *Shadows Need Light*."

Myles passed along two dessert dishes with slices of coconut flan. Alessandro handed her one. "Do you like me in person, though?"

He was more beautiful on the big screen, but much more interesting to look at in real life. Either way, she liked him just fine. Still, it was more fun to tease him. "You know what they say about meeting your heroes."

He narrowed his eyes at her. "Should I be flattered you ever considered me a hero, or disappointed I fell short of your expectations?"

Angel wasn't disappointed. She was well fed and having an amazing time. "You met my expectations," she said. "And thanks for dinner. It was awesome."

"It's not over. Try the flan."

It turned out to be the best advice. The flan was light, creamy and delicious. "I know you're a big movie star and everything, but how did you get Myles Paquin to cook your dinner? I can never get a reservation at his restaurant."

"Myles? He's my cousin!"

"Oh?"

She stared at the chef but could not pick up a trace of familial resemblance. Myles was the color of brown sugar with long, thick, wavy hair that deserved its own social media channel. Still, she wasn't so closed-minded to rule out their family ties. "Are you a clan of prodigies, by any chance?"

He licked the back of his fork. "More like a clan of delinquents. We grew up on the same block. His mother is my 'aunt,' just not really."

"And you're still close after all these years?"

"I can't shake him loose."

Angel was envious. She did not have a bench of childhood friends to call up at a pinch. It was her fault, for spending most of her free time in her artist's studio. And by studio, she meant her bedroom.

After the plates were cleared away, DJ Jordan was the first to leave. Despite his occupation, or maybe because of it, he was an early sleeper. "Peace, bro!" he shouted on his way out.

"Peace!" Alessandro called back.

Shortly thereafter, Rose picked up her miniscule purse and announced that she and Jenny were heading out. She was a stunning black woman, long and lanky. She wore her hair braided in neat rows gathered at the nape of her neck. Her accent was decidedly French.

"Cool meeting you," she said to Angel. "Love your name, by the way. Is it short for Angela, Angelica, Angelina…?"

"Angeline." The name had been in her family for generations.

"That's French!" she exclaimed. *"Tu parles Français?"*

Angel had to focus to generate a somewhat decent answer. *"Un peu... Je suis Haitienne...mais Americaine."*

"Je suis Marocaine," Rose said with a laugh. "Don't worry. I won't torture you with any more French." She planted a kiss on Alessandro's forehead. "We're still on for tomorrow."

Alessandro joined his hands behind his head. "We'll see."

"Oh, don't start!" Jenny scolded. She draped an arm around her girlfriend's waist. "Gigi will be here tomorrow and she'll set you straight."

Rose beckoned to Myles, who was absently scrolling through his phone. "Hey you! We might as well take the same ferry off Fantasy Island."

"I don't ferry," Myles said. "I have my boat."

Rose and Jenny rejoiced.

"Aren't you suddenly more attractive!" Rose cried.

"It's not a yacht," Myles warned.

"Never mind yachts," Jenny said. "Let's go!"

The three headed inside the penthouse, calling out, "Ciao!"

"Kisses!"

"Later!"

Alessandro waved goodbye to his friends. "Get outta here! Be safe!"

Angel watched them go. They could not have been more obvious. Alessandro's friends were clearing out to give him space to...what?

"They know their way out," he said. "You don't have to look so concerned."

She was concerned, only not for them.

He studied her in his quiet way. "Let's play a game. Up for it?"

The only game she ought to play was one that resulted

in her transferring ownership of an oil painting and him transferring funds into the gallery's account. Win-win. Angel wasn't so green as to ignore the timeworn principle: no deal was done until money had exchanged hands.

Maybe it was the food, the wine, the flan and the whole dolce vita vibe, but yeah…she was up for it.

"You tell me one secret or embarrassing thing about yourself, and I'll do the same. It doesn't have to cut deep. You don't have to unearth a childhood trauma. Just something. Okay?"

She reached for her wineglass. This game did not sound fun. "You go first."

"Okay," he said. "When I was fifteen I stole a car, stripped its tires and sold them in under an hour. I used the money to buy a PlayStation."

The look on her face must have given him ample ammunition to come after her. "God, I can't believe you bought that!"

"It's not true?"

"No way!"

In her defense, he'd established the rules. "This is a bluffing game?"

"I never stole a car," he said. "I've never stolen anything. I went to a high school for performing arts and did community theatre!"

"What's the point of this game?"

"I know what I look like and what people think when they see me."

His view must be distorted because from where she sat, he was *Temptation*. "Community theatre?" she said, trying to make light of the whole thing. "You're losing street cred in my eyes."

"I'll take that chance." He paused "You're safe with me, if that's what you're wondering."

How could Angel make him understand? A man's penthouse apartment did not rank high on the designated safe spaces for women. Either way, her unease wasn't rooted in fear. She needed clear boundaries, signs, guideposts, a rulebook and adult supervision to be alone with him.

"That's not what I'm wondering," she said.

"What then?"

"To be or not to be?"

He laughed. "What?"

"You're not the only one who's dabbled in theatre."

"So we have that in common," he said. His voice was rich and sweet and he served it up like coconut flan.

Angel studied him openly. This man had poured her wine, fed her heirloom tomatoes and left the table to retrieve clean utensils when she'd dropped her fork. She'd been convinced that he was showing off for his friends. Now, though, his audience had cleared out. They were alone and he was not letting up. Alessandro Cardenas was still flirting with her, and she did not know how to deal.

"Alright," she said. "I'll confess to something bad."

His gaze flickered. "You? Angel? *No me digas.*"

"When I was fourteen, I stole blue nail polish at a dollar store."

"Wait a minute," he said. "I confessed to grand auto theft. That's a felony in some states. And you give me dollar store nail polish?"

"You confessed to nothing!" she fired back. "And FYI: I wasn't shocked at your made-up juvenile delinquency."

He tilted his head and peered at her through his long, thick lashes. "No?"

"I promise," she said. "I wasn't prepared, that's all. You said no childhood trauma."

He leaned back in his chair. His shirt gaped open. That smooth expanse of skin was just an arm's length away.

"I said it to reassure you. You looked so scared."

"If I look *scared*, it's because I'm way off course here!" she snapped. "I'm on the clock. And yet, here I am, out here, playing games with you!"

She could get fired for this. When celebrities stopped by the gallery, the sales staff was never allowed to get too close. They were supposed to maintain an attitude of professional indifference at all times.

"And yet, here you are playing games with me," Alessandro repeated, as if the actor in him could not resist the chance to pump her words for full dramatic effect.

His eyes lingered on her face. For the first time that night, Angel heard the soft murmur of the surf. It had always been there beneath their chatter and laughter. The question she'd been truly turning in her mind bobbed to the surface. She dared to say it.

"Why does it feel like you don't want me to go?"

His gaze flickered, a ripple in the sea. "Because I don't."

Angel exhaled, feeling better with it all out in the open. But he looked pensive. He stood up and extended a hand. "Come on. I'll buy your painting and take you home."

Her heart sank. He'd come to a conclusion about her. What was it? That she was too small town to play at his level, too uptight, too *scared*. But wasn't she all those things?

She ignored his outstretched hand and stood on her own. The time for fun and games was over.

"You're under no obligation to buy it," she said. "You haven't even seen it."

"I'm familiar with it."

The case with the painting was where Angel had left it. If anyone had walked off with it, her boss would have sold her on the black market to recoup the cost. He sat on the arm of one of the two suede cloudlike couches. Under his watchful gaze, she punched in the pin, released the lock, and reached in for the eight-by-ten-inch framed oil painting. "As requested: *El Jardín Secreto* by Juan David Valero."

The small painting wasn't as pretentious as *Temptation*. Did it merit a *Miami Vice* sunset speedboat trip across the bay for an in-person delivery? Maybe not. Juan David Valero was a respected but obscure artist from Cuba who had passed away decades ago. Very few high-profile collectors were clamoring for his work.

Earlier, Angel's boss had sent her a prepared statement via text message. She pulled out her phone and read it aloud.

"The midcentury Cuban artist is best known for his renderings of daily life in 1950s Havana."

She glanced at Alessandro to gauge his reaction. The set of his jaw led her to abandon the prepared statement. She pocketed her phone. "It's no *diptych*," she said. "But I love that the artist's only ambition was to share a tender memory."

His expression softened. Encouraged, Angel continued. "The artist renders landscapes in muted shades of green and yellow and blue. That's unusual in Caribbean art, which is usually bursting with color. Valero was a Cuban exile. I believe he used color to communicate his nostalgia."

"He was depressed," Alessandro said flatly.

Angel studied the little painting with new eyes. The garden was bursting with red bougainvillea, but always tucked away in the shade. All the beauty in the world was veiled in darkness. "It's possible. I'll admit I'm not too familiar with this artist's body of work."

"It's fine."

It was not fine. She would have done her homework if she'd had the time. "I'm standing in for Justine Carr. It was all very last minute and—"

"Angel, trust me. It's fine," he said.

"Alright." She handed him the canvas and, to her disappointment, he placed it on a side table without so much as a glance.

"Why do you even want it?" It was such a modest painting, so unlike the artwork on display in the house.

His gaze slid down her body, liquid and hot. "We want what we want."

"I want a straight answer."

"You got one."

Angel took a breath. Her job wasn't to talk the client out of the sale. "We're asking forty-five grand."

"And that's what you'll get."

In her opinion, he was overpaying by ten grand. But he hadn't asked her opinion. Plus, in the spirit of Art Basel, overpaying for stuff was part of the fun. He reached for his phone and completed the transfer of funds. She received email confirmation. Her boss sent her a text message with a thumbs-up emoji. She handed over the envelope with the bill of sale and certificate of authentication. It joined the painting on the table.

Angel could now confirm that reports of Alessandro Cardenas's appreciation for art were greatly exaggerated. He was likely collecting random pieces for the same reasons rich people did anything: the tax break. *El Jardín Secreto* would probably end up buried in Freeport art storage in Delaware.

"We're done," she said.

"Seems so," he said. "But what's the matter? You don't look happy."

She snapped the case shut. "I'm thrilled."

"You don't look it."

"It's just...art is personal to me," she said. "I understand that for some it's strictly an investment."

He steepled his fingers. "Go on."

"I'd prefer to sell you a piece that would..." She grappled for the right word. "I don't know..."

"Spark joy?"

His snarky tone pissed her off. "Yes! Pinwheels of joy! Why not?"

He grinned. "It's sparking something!"

That devious grin! It poked out when you least expected it, like the sun in a rainstorm. She had to drop this. What did it matter if he loved the painting or not? Whether he sold it on eBay or hung it in his bathroom, it was none of her business.

Her phone buzzed in her dress pocket. Angel reached for it, needing an excuse to look away. There was a chance it was a text from her boss with a follow-up question. It wasn't.

NEW POST ALERT! @CHRIS_UNDERWATER posted a new video to his channel: DEEP DIVE, A FRESHWATER EXPLORATION

Angel stared at the screen. Eyes stinging, she swiped away the alert. She was suddenly furious with herself. Her ex was off living his best aquatic life. Here she was with a man who was making it very plain that he wanted to dive into her body. All she could do was think up excuses to say no. Is this who she wanted to be? The woman who rushed home to popcorn, boxed wine and YouTube? The woman who, decades from now, would sit on a rocker and tell her knitting circle about the night she'd met a handsome movie star and was too much of a mouse to make a move? She was worried about losing her job, too, only that didn't seem as important anymore.

Alessandro fished a set of keys from a copper bowl on the coffee table. "I'll take you home."

"No."

He went still. "No?"

"I'm in no hurry."

A series of unusual events had landed her here tonight. She'd stay and explore every avenue. Tomorrow she'd walk away, *run* away. But tonight, she'd play the role, be whomever she needed to be to take this chance.

Three

If Sandro believed in divine intervention and the like, he would have thought his grandfather had sent him an angel to guide him. Not the kind who comes in peace, but the other kind.

Earlier, his driver had called to inform him that the gallery rep was on the way up. Then his housekeeper texted: Ángel is here. Sandro and his friends had returned from a swim. He'd thought nothing of grabbing his rumpled shirt off the back of his chair and racing in from the terrace. He came skidding to a stop when he saw her. In her white dress and standing just where the sunlight slid across the terrazzo floor, there was something unearthly about her. Her honey-brown skin was aglow and her windswept hair, dark and wavy, had spun sunshine into a halo around her head. She looked up from the paintings that she'd been studying and fixed her steady, light-filled eyes on him.

Angel…short for Angeline.

He had no choice but to revisit his stance on divine intervention.

She had wanted to get straight down to business and wasted no time presenting the case with the painting he'd requested. He hadn't wanted her to open that case. Like a ticking time bomb, it had the potential of blowing up everything. Instead, he'd asked her to stay for dinner.

Sandro lived a YOLO lifestyle in Los Angeles; it was the Hollywood way. Now or never. Maybe he'd forgotten how to be around normal people. People who didn't jump into bed with the first attractive person they met. Unfortunately, they didn't have the time to get to know each other better. He was in town for only a few nights. On Monday he was flying back to California to start rehearsals for his next film. Sandro had come home to relax and hang with friends, not to find a lover. Since he'd laid eyes on Angel, he'd wanted to know if that option was on the table.

Now she wanted to stay. At last, the opening he'd been waiting for and, for some reason, he was hesitant. It came back to his first impression: she was a normal person, here to do a job. Shouldn't he leave her alone?

Take the gifts of this hour. That was his motto. *Just take it!* All night, he'd been so impatient to touch her, to feel all that glowing brown skin. If she could light him up with just a look from across a room, he wondered what other tricks she could do. He wanted his other senses satisfied. Touch, taste, smell—yes, he wanted her scent on his hands. But he couldn't overlook the glaring signs hinting that something was wrong.

He pointed to her phone. "What was that?"

She feigned innocence. "What was what?"

"That message upset you. It's obvious."

She shoved the phone into a pocket of her dress, as if

to bury the evidence. "It was my alarm, reminding me of something I no longer have to do."

This angel was a little liar. "I should have asked if someone was waiting for you at home."

"No one is waiting for me anywhere."

"In that case..." He dropped his keys into the bowl. Then he led her back outside, not to the terrace where they'd had dinner but to the rooftop deck with its bar, lap pool, hot tub, outdoor shower and endless views. He pulled a fresh bottle from the stocked wine cooler beneath the bar, and poured two generous glasses of God-knows-what. They went to stand by the balustrade, facing the night.

"You have the best views," she said.

It was a quiet night. Sandro turned his back to the view and admired her instead. Tousled hair, eyes like topaz, lips wet with wine, he liked this view better.

"I had my eye on this place for a while," he said. "Bought it days after I signed a major endorsement deal. The sad truth is that I don't get to spend more than two weeks at a time here. I'm either in LA or on set. Most of the time my niece crashes here."

"I want to pity you," she said with a smile. "But it's so damn hard."

"Not looking for pity," he said. "I'm trying to tell you something."

She took a sip of wine. "What's that?"

He was momentarily distracted by the way the delicate gold chain she wore pooled at her collar. He yearned to lean in and kiss that spot. And for the first time all night he suspected that she might want him to. Before he did anything, Sandro had to make a few things clear.

"This trip will be shorter than most and I'll be gone in a few days."

She glanced up at him sharply. "Why would I need to know this?"

"Because I want you to have all the facts." Sandro wanted her to come out of her shell and play, but only if it felt right. "There's an upside: nothing you do or say tonight will matter. You can throw caution to the wind."

"First of all, everything matters. Second, what do you think I'm doing here?"

She pressed a palm to her chest as if to attest that her presence on his rooftop deck was proof positive she'd stepped so far out on a ledge she could not take one more step.

Sandro wasn't buying it. He pointed to the phone she'd hidden away. "I think you're hiding the truth in your pocket."

She let her head roll back out of sheer weariness. And this time, he could not restrain himself. "May I touch you?"

She gave him a hard look. He expected her to throw the contents of her wineglass in his face and he braced himself. To his relief, she nodded.

He leaned in and kissed where the thin gold chain grazed her collar. She didn't pull away. Instead, she brought the flat of her palm to his cheek, keeping him close.

"You can talk to me, Angel," he whispered against her warm skin. "I won't tell anyone."

"You'll judge," she whispered back.

She was trembling.

Sandro buried his nose in the hollow of her neck. "You don't know me. I don't judge."

"And I'll never know you," she said. "Isn't that the point? In a few days, you'll be gone."

"In a few days, you'll have forgotten me."

"Do people forget the great Alessandro Cardenas?"

He pulled away from her and leaned against the balustrade. "When he's not putting on a performance, they do."

"Ah!" she exclaimed, as if she'd spotted the North Star or something.

"What is it?"

"It just hit me! I can be whomever I want and you can be yourself. Win-win."

Clever. He hadn't thought about it that way. "I like the sound of that."

She let out a shaky breath and when she spoke her voice was as fragile as a blade of grass. "My ex-boyfriend followed his bliss halfway around the world. Now he posts about his adventures on YouTube."

"You loved him?"

With so much to unpack, why had that been his first question?

"I used to."

"What's his bliss?"

"Marine biology, specifically coral ecology."

Sandro couldn't even diss the guy. The coral reefs were in peril and the jerk was doing something about it.

"I followed him from Central Florida to Miami so he could wrap up research for his PhD. Then he packed up for Australia for a postdoc residency."

"And left you behind."

"Something like that."

Sandro did not want to know the answer to his next question, yet he had to ask. "Was that message from him just now?"

She moved away from him, walking backward. "If I were just dodging his messages, there'd be nothing to be embarrassed about."

He went after her. "Embarrassed? Now I need to know."

"Alright!" She took another sip of wine. "So I mentioned he started a YouTube channel. I get alerts each time he posts a new video."

Sandro barked out a laugh. "You little stalker!"

Her jaw dropped. "That's *not* what I'm doing!"

"That's exactly what you're doing."

"No!"

"Yes, my angel," he said. "You're cyberstalking your ex."

She groaned and pressed the wineglass to her forehead.

He took the glass from her and used the rim to raise her chin. "Admitting you have a problem is the first step to recovery."

"Oh, shut up!" She swatted him away. "It's just… He's exploring caves and sampling lagers… I don't know. His life seemed so interesting. Maybe I was keeping tabs."

"Hey! We've all been there."

"Really? Who have you stalked recently?"

Sandro shook his head. "In the interest of privacy, we won't name names."

She stared wide-eyed at him. "Interesting."

"Not really." In recent years, he'd learned to cut his losses. Which was what Angel had to learn.

She absently slid off her shoes and immediately lost a few inches. He wanted to fall at her feet.

"Since you're an expert, what's the next step?" she said. "Aside from the usual blocking, unfollowing and deleting the app."

"All good precautions," he said. "What are your thoughts on rebound sex?"

She coughed. The nervous little sound echoed in the night. "I'm neither for nor against it."

"That's the cure," he teased. "Give it some thought."

Sandro walked over to the bar and set their glasses in

the sink. She was hung up on her ex. Did he want to get mixed up in that? On the other hand, what did it matter to him? *If he followed his own logic, in a few days none of this would matter.*

Everything matters.

Angel stood with her hands in her pockets. "Are you offering your…services?"

He went to her and leaned close. This time he kissed the corner of her mouth. "When you put it like that, it sounds as dirty as it should be."

She went perfectly still. He breathed in her sweet floral perfume and he had his answer. He wanted to get mixed up in whatever this was.

"I wouldn't say no," she said.

That was a start. "I need you to say yes."

She took one step closer and whispered her answer. "Yes."

When Alessandro Cardenas offered sex, even obliquely, you said yes and dealt with the fallout later. That was only common sense. Right?

In a restroom off the pool deck, Angel was having a moment. She splashed water on her neck to cool down. She could lose her job over this. If word got out that she slept with clients, what other reputable gallery would have her? Her professional reputation would be destroyed before she had a chance to build it up. Angel dabbed her face and neck with a towel as these thoughts assailed her. Then her fingers lingered at the spot that he had kissed and, just like that, she was on fire again. There was no way she was backing out.

It wasn't like she hadn't considered rebound sex before he'd offered it. It was item No. 5 of her five-point plan to get over Chris. *#5 Get back on the saddle.* Only she hadn't even made it to *#2 Reconnect with old friends*. So this felt like jumping the gun. Then again, item No. 1 was to follow her bliss, and this oddly fit the bill.

God, but when he kissed her…the way he said her name…there was no way she could have said no.

For now, they were going for a swim.

Angel tied her hair in a topknot and stripped off her clothes. After a quick consultation in the mirror, she let out a resigned sigh. A runner since high school, her body was strong with a fair amount of curves. Right now, though, she might've regretted gorging on Chef Myles's food if it hadn't been so damn delicious! In a rattan basket, Angel found a collection of swimsuits, all new with tags. Alessandro had explained that his niece was a travel blogger/ social media influencer and received tons of free clothes, some she made available for last-minute guests. She picked a one-size-fits-most black bikini with string ties, slipped it on and headed out the door before she lost her nerve.

He was nowhere to be found. The rooftop deck was deserted. She walked over to the pool's edge and for a minute she imagined him hanging out with his friends, lazily worshiping the sun while the others laughed and splashed around. The sound of pouring water caught her attention. She followed it to a manmade waterfall tucked away in an alcove. And there he was, naked, leaning forward with a hand pressed to the stone-paved wall as water rushed down the mountainous terrain of his back. She didn't have to imagine anything anymore.

She did not dare move.

He spotted her anyway and stepped out of the water stream. "Found everything you needed?"

She nodded.

He reached out and rested a hand on her hip. It was warm and wet and she didn't realize until too late that he was tugging at the string holding the bikini bottom together.

"And you thought you'd need this?" One sharp tug and the bit of triangular fabric fell away. He then worked on the strings tied below her shoulder blades and lifted the bikini top over her head. "You won't need this, either."

Her heart thundered in her chest as he guided her into the shower. He held her by the waist under the heavy stream. Water poured down her back and between her breasts. He drew her to him, kissed her then gently eased her back into the stream, letting the rush of water do its job. The pressure beat down on her. He drew her to him once again and smoothed back her hair. Angel had to blink to see clearly. His face was inches from hers. Drops of water clung to his lashes and shone like glass beads. She had no idea what other people thought when they saw him, but she thought he was devastatingly beautiful.

Inhibitions thoroughly washed away, Angel mingled her fingers with his and guided his hand between her thighs. Water poured down their bodies, but she wanted him to discover the wetness there. His touch made her delirious. She shut her eyes and tipped backward.

He drew her back and held her tight. "Stay close."

Angel whimpered. He pressed a kiss to her ear and, voice gruff, murmured, "What do you need?"

More of this! All of this! Warm water, cool breeze, moonlight, his touch, all of it! Those words were crammed in her throat. She couldn't speak.

He gathered her hair and tugged on it. "Talk to me."

"I need you."

Oh, girl... What had just come out of her mouth?

There was no time for regrets. He crushed them all with his kiss.

Four

With a hop, skip and a jump, Angel had landed in bed with a notorious Hollywood heartthrob. The chorus of internal voices that had egged her on last night wasted no time shaming her in the morning. She'd obviously lost her mind. Had she risked her job for a one-night stand? She'd let a sweet-talking celebrity turn her head. The man had flown down from California to party all weekend and she'd offered herself up as a favor!

These thoughts invaded her mind before she even opened her eyes. It was 6:00 a.m. She knew it without having to consult her phone or watch. Angel woke up every morning at six, often to start her day with a quick run or to prep a canvas for later that night. It had been months since she'd done either of those things, yet the habit remained. Alessandro was sleeping beside her, his breath crashing in even waves. Angel listened, her own breath rising and falling, keeping time with his.

She was wading in dangerous waters. The sounds of his breath, his warmth, his leg thrown over hers, the citrusy scent of his sheets—together they had the force of an emotional riptide strong enough to pull her under. She wanted to cuddle close to him and fall back asleep. Maybe later he'd wake her with demanding kisses.

She wanted to do it all again.

For that precise reason, she had to get the hell out.

Running had always been part of her hastily hashed plan. Putting the plan in motion was tricky. She hadn't thought it would be this elaborate, a hug and a quick kiss goodbye at 2:00 a.m. at most. But after they'd made love on his bedroom floor, he'd scooped her up and carried her to bed. She'd plunged into a deep sleep.

Thanks to top-notch blackout drapes, the room was plunged in darkness. Without risking a glance at her bed partner, Angel slipped out from under the sheets. Where had she left her dress? And her shoes? All she had within reach was the large white towel he'd wrapped around her body before they took off running from the rooftop deck to his bedroom for quick access to his stash of condoms. The towel lay crumpled now on the wood floor as a cruel reminder of just how *fun* last night had been, how much more fun they could have this morning if she could bring herself to stay.

Stick to the plan.

Angel grabbed the towel, wrapped it around her body and tiptoed out of the room. She hesitated a while, her hand on the knob, her forehead pressed to the closed door. Privately she thanked him, wished him luck and said goodbye.

It was better this way, and by "better" she meant "easier" on her.

Angel turned away from the door and toward more

practical matters. Finding her clothes would require no less than a scavenger hunt. She'd changed out of her dress in the rooftop restroom, but had stepped out of her heels well before that. Where had she left them? She gingerly made her way down the hall to the main living area. Which way to the roof? She couldn't remember. And how would she even get off this damn island? It wasn't as if she could order an Uber.

Help arrived in the form of the housekeeper. At this early hour, she was humming to herself while watering a bird of paradise in a massive white planter. She turned from her task. The look she gave Angel loosely translated into, *"¡Ay pobrecita!"*

"Good morning," Angel said, her dignity in shreds.

"Come," she replied. "I have everything you need."

Her name was Maritza. She'd gone on the scavenger hunt and collected Angel's things, including the metal case that she'd forgotten all about. It cost north of two hundred dollars and the gallery would have taken it out of her salary.

Burning with equal parts gratitude and humiliation, Angel changed in a powder room off the foyer. When she emerged, she asked Maritza how she might catch the ferry.

"I can arrange for a driver to meet you in the lobby. Is that okay?"

Angel was dangerously close to tears. "That's great. Thank you so much. For everything."

Maritza escorted her to the elevator and left Angel with a pat to her shoulder.

A golf cart ride to the marina, a race along the dock to catch the ferry already pulling away, a quick leap on board, and Angel had made it out of paradise. She took a seat on a wood banquette and kept her gaze fixed on the Miami skyline. Her fellow passengers were properly dressed and likely returning home from night shifts as nannies and security guards. Out of respect, Angel resisted breaking into hysterical laughter.

It had been a night of firsts. First one-night stand… with a celebrity. First time she'd ever ducked out on a man without so much as a kiss goodbye. First orgasm in an outdoor shower, which was a weirdly specific category but nonetheless true. First full night's sleep since Chris's departure. First time she'd opened up about Chris to anyone.

Angel hadn't confided in anyone about the breakup, mostly because she'd lost touch with most of the friends she'd left behind in Orlando. As for family, that was dicey. Her older sister, Bernadette, was judgmental as hell. Newly married, she had cautioned Angel not to trail after Chris to Miami. *He won't marry you*, she'd proclaimed, as if marriage were the ultimate goal in life. When news of their breakup got out, Bernadette had wasted no time sending an "I told you so" text.

She hadn't gone into details with Alessandro, but it had felt good to release the pressure valve. Chris Moyer, a native of landlocked Nebraska with a lifelong fascination with the sea. This had led him to Florida to study marine biology. A native Floridian, Angel had always taken the beaches for granted. She and Chris had met in graduate school. He was pursuing a doctorate; she was wrapping up an MFA. Theirs was an opposites attract sort of thing, but they truly could not have been more different. A pragmatic guy with single-minded focus, Chris had never aligned with Angel's fluid views on life and career. He had short- and long-term goals that extended into the next decade or two. Angel could not see too far into the future and took each day as it came. In the end, though, this attitude hadn't served her and she was actively working to change.

On her thirtieth birthday two things happened. Angel could not get a reservation at *Diablo* and a gallery turned her down for a group exhibition. Chris had patiently waited until the next day to announce that he had accepted a post-doctorate position in Australia and didn't think it was a good idea for her to come along. "This was fun," he'd said, dismissing three years of a committed relationship with three one-syllable words.

This. Was. Fun.

Fun was dinner under the stars, playing bluffing games, talking to the point of revealing too much, holding back only to spill everything out with no regrets. Fun was a first kiss under a manmade waterfall followed by a mad race to the bedroom on bare, slippery feet.

Angel lowered her head in her hands. Bernadette was right. The last thing she needed was fun. Her fun career in the arts was a flop. The fun ride of her last relationship had ended in a ditch. For the sake of her sanity, all the fun she'd had last night had to be shelved away.

In a few days, you'll forget me.

Oh, how she wished that were true.

Five

Angel was gone. Sandro woke up sure of it.

He shot up, sent the sheets flying and scrambled out of bed. In a move that ended up saving him time, he yanked back the thick curtains to let in some light. From his bedroom, he could see as far as the marina. He caught sight of her tiny frame racing barefoot along the dock, shoes cradled in her arms, hair in the wind.

This little angel is bad.

He watched the ferry fade into the distance and sighed. It was for the best. Sandro had an eye for beauty, and sometimes it led him astray. Right now he couldn't afford the distraction. He was on a mission in Miami, an unpleasant one that required a level head. Yet, as distractingly beautiful as Angel was, she had not wasted his time. She had delivered the painting and the certificate of authenticity that wasn't worth the card stock it was printed on.

It surprised him that for all her keen-eyed observations,

she was clueless regarding the nature of her errand. She had not connected the dots between him and the artist Juan David Valero. Sandro liked her all the more for it.

Alessandro David Cardenas was the grandson of Juan David Valero. His favorite grandson, by all accounts. At his death, Sandro had inherited the bulk of his paintings. A fire had destroyed half and Alessandro made it his mission to preserve the rest. He had repurchased anything he could find on the market, which wasn't much. His grandfather had not been, by any stretch, a commercial success. And yet new pieces kept cropping up. It wasn't until a friend had very proudly unveiled a Valero original purchased while on a fishing trip in Miami that Sandro began to suspect these new pieces were fakes. The painting of the Havana Harbor at dusk had all the trappings of his late grandfather's work—the broad brushstrokes and the muted color palette that Angel had so beautifully described—but there was something "off" about it. That was all he could say. Sandro's friend, a Cuban attorney from New Jersey, had all the best intentions. He had not wanted to embarrass the guy, so he kept his suspicions to himself. He did get the name of the Lincoln Road art gallery that had sold him the painting and made some inquiries.

What role, if any, did Angeline Louis play in this? None, he'd decided, and shut the door to any doubts.

Sandro went to the old wood desk that used to belong to his grandfather, flipped open a notebook and drew her face from memory with an ink pen. He did not want to forget her. He sketched her angular face, almond-shaped eyes, flared nose, and heart-shaped mouth. What that mouth had done to him…

He dropped the pen, the memories flooding back. The attraction between them had been there, whole and intact, the instant they'd met. He thought her beautiful from the start, but once she had started describing his grandfather's work, from the muted color palette to the emotional undertones, he found her riveting.

The scripted speech had irritated him. He'd held the hands that had mixed those paints and didn't need a lecture. Still, he'd appreciated the way she went on to present his *abuelo* as a person, not merely a signature on a canvas. She'd looked for nuance and meaning in the composition, color palette and even the brush strokes. Then he'd reminded himself that what she was so poetically describing was in all likelihood a cheap fake. His reaction had upset her. He liked that she cared so much.

He just liked her.

For all her good intentions, Angel was wrong about his grandfather whom she'd painted as a romantic figure, struck with nostalgia—the classic affliction of the Cuban exile. Juan David, JD to the family, had fled Castro's Cuba in 1970, leaving behind his country, his family, and a fiancée whom he loved. That was certainly enough to cripple any man. It took years for Sandro to acknowledge the deeper truth: his grandfather was flat out depressed. He would have benefited from therapy and medication if his machismo hadn't prevented him from seeking help.

It certainly didn't help that the old man felt like a failure. Having dedicated his life to his art, JD never made a penny from it. And that was why Sandro was determined to prevent anyone from exploiting his work after his death. He would protect his legacy no matter what.

Sandro slipped on shorts, grabbed his phone and went to the kitchen for coffee. Maritza was there and had already poured him a cup. She was spooky like that.

She put the cup on the island counter before him. "Your friend is gone."

"Ah!" he said. So that's how she'd managed it, with Maritza's help.

"She is a very nice girl, very pretty, very polite."

There was a not-so-subtle reproach in her voice. "And I'm not nice?"

"You are a Hollywood playboy."

Did she think he'd kicked the very pretty, very polite girl out of bed? "She left me! I was sleeping and she took off. *You* helped her."

Maritza joined her hands as if in prayer. "I am not telling you how to live your life. I only said that she is a nice girl."

"Who's a nice girl? You can't mean me." His niece, Sabina, entered the kitchen. She was wearing the same outfit that she'd worn when she'd left the day before. "What did I miss? Did Tío have a girl over?"

"Good morning," Sandro said. "And never mind that."

Maritza poured Sabina a cup of coffee and discretely backed out of the kitchen. He had the suspicion that his housekeeper didn't think his niece was "nice."

Sabina stirred sugar in her coffee and confronted him. "What's that in the living room?"

"What's what?" Sandro asked.

She brushed a lock of black hair away from her face. "The painting by JD. Where did you get it?"

Sabina was his half brother Eddy's daughter, but she looked more and more like her mother who had tragically passed away when she was twelve. Eddy had since remarried and moved to Tampa. Sabina did not get along with her stepmom and stayed on Fisher Island whenever she was in Miami. Her official occupation was travel blogger.

Sandro put down his mug. "Why do you need to know?"

Sabina continued her interrogation. "Why did you buy it? What's your plan? To put it away with the others?"

The "others" were in storage, except for the few in his LA home. "Does that bother you?"

"Art is supposed to be on display for people to love and admire," she said. "JD wouldn't want you to hoard his work like that."

He wasn't hoarding anything. And what would she know about it? His grandfather died two years after she was born. "If you have so many strong opinions, why don't you paint yourself? You used to back when you were in high school."

"I used to pole dance back in high school, too," she said. "For the exercise."

Sandro sipped his coffee. This conversation had taken an odd turn.

"Daddy thinks it's selfish of you to hide JD's work, and I agree."

So it was *Daddy* now? She hadn't called her father that in a while. Interesting that his niece's change of heart coincided with the one time that she and Eddy were taking sides against him.

"So I'm selfish," Sandro said. "I can live with that."

She slammed down her tiny spoon. "You're a big deal now! Why not use your platform to promote his work? Let people discover it. You'd be surprised how much they'd pay—"

"No."

"Okay," she said. "If you're not interested, let me try. I'll never be as big as you but—"

"No."

As the eldest grandchild, Eddy had happily inherited their grandfather's fishing boat. Sandro had inherited the valueless art. There had been no formal reading of a will, but as boys they'd agreed to this. The boat had been sold for scraps years ago. The art, however, would outlast them all.

"Why?" Sabina snapped. "You do it for your friends? Why not your family?"

"What are you talking about?"

"Myles's restaurant! Jordan's DJ gigs! You promoted them and they blew up!"

If he were petty, he'd add her travel blogging career to that list. "I don't promote them. I attend their events on my own time. I can't help it if my friends are talented."

"So what do you call going live on Instagram at *Diablo*'s grand opening or at Club TENTEN when Jordan has a set?"

"I call it living my life." What would be the point of promoting his grandfather's paintings? He had no intention of selling them. His hope was to pass them on to his kids… and his niece. Anyway, it was much too early for this conversation. "Sabina, I can't deal with you right now."

"You won't have to. I'm only here to pack a bag."

He had been looking forward to spending time with her today. "Don't go. You just got here."

"Don't take it personally. It's work. Soho House is hosting influencers this weekend for Art Week. And spare me the sad puppy eyes. Sounds like you won't be lonely." She grabbed a banana from the fruit bowl Maritza kept full and swirled out of the kitchen. "Catch you later, Tío!"

Sandro felt the stab of heartburn. This day wasn't supposed to have started with him arguing with his niece over his grandfather's paintings, and no amount of coffee was going to fix that. It should have begun in bed with Angel. But he'd been cheated of that experience and it was making him cranky. There was no other way to put it, really. He'd been cheated.

The door to Sabina's bedroom slammed shut. What was

he going to do about the growing gulf between him and his family? He hated to draw this parallel, but since bringing home the Oscar two years back, his relationships with his few remaining family members had deteriorated. His brother rarely called and now he was filling Sabina's head with ideas. It saddened him. With his father long dead and two-thirds of his relatives back in Cuba, many he would likely never meet, Sandro didn't take family for granted.

His phone buzzed with a text message. He welcomed the distraction. At least he could always count on his friends. Georgina Garcia, better known as Gigi, was the daughter of a former Dominican baseball star. Sandro was lucky to count the trust fund baby–turned–film studio head as one of his best friends. He had worked on one of her first projects and his performance had earned her studio its first Independent Spirit Award. It had also gotten him a meeting with the director of *Shadows Need Light*, the biopic of Cuban cinematographer and activist Néstor Almendros. He'd cinched the role of Julio, one of Néstor's lovers and a fellow gay rights activist.

Gigi was in Miami for the same reason everyone was in Miami. The text message read:

Tonight's itinerary: Cocktails at Pérez Museum, Basel event for one hour tops, dinner at the Mandarin and afterparty at the Aston Martin Residences. Are you in? Or are you in???

Sandro was about to reply when his agent, Leslie Chapman, called with the classic combo of good news and bad news. A standoff between the director of his next film and the production company had resulted in more setbacks. Rehearsals were delayed until after the holidays.

"What's the problem?" he asked. This was meant to

be his first big budget fantasy movie in which he played
a space pilot.

"Money is the problem."

"What's the good news?"

"You've got some time off," she said. "Yay!"

"Come on, Leslie! What am I going to do with time
off?"

Sandro knew that most people didn't react this way to
the prospect of free time. However, he wasn't wired like
most people. He worked. That's what he did. Day in, day
out, around the clock, he worked. On short breaks like
this one, which were few and far between, he connected
with friends and partied hard. That was how he liked it.
Everything in balance.

"For God's sake, man! You're home on a private island
in Miami. I'd trade places with you in a heartbeat. Plus it's
December and before you know it, the—"

"The holidays? If you tell me to spend time with my
family, so help me—"

"Boy, please!" Leslie cried. "I was going to say the
Golden Globe nominations are around the corner. I've
got a good feeling. Take some time to relax. It's going to
be wild after that."

It was Leslie's job to dream big. Sandro had no reason-
able expectation of a Golden Globe nomination for his supporting role in a series that had aired on a new streaming
platform. He'd been snubbed for the Emmy, after all. That
didn't bother him too much. His pride in his work wasn't
contingent on winning a gold statue. Leslie was right on
one point: he *was* home. A little solitude wouldn't kill
him. There was the pool, and if not the pool, the beach.
And Angel… Don't forget Angel…

"I'll send you scripts to read and look out for a television appearance on a holiday special. Or maybe a late-

night talk show. How about Fallon? Would that cheer you up?"

"Don't bother," he said. "I'm going to take your advice."

Leslie hollered over the line. "Am I dreaming or what?"

"It wouldn't kill me to slow down."

"Damn straight! And I like to keep my clients busy. You know my motto."

Sandro chanted, "You make money, I make money."

"And we all go home happy, baby!" Leslie chimed. "Except today I recommend that you *stop* working. Just. Stop. There's such a thing as burnout."

As a black woman in Hollywood, Leslie understood the business better than most. She knew how hard it was to break past stereotypes and score the types of roles that got an actor noticed. Sandro was a trained actor, but he would have been stuck playing the bad boy boyfriend or "some kind of Latino" for life if he hadn't signed with Leslie. Now that his career was on track, he was in a strike-the-iron-while-it's-hot frame of mind. When you came from a long line of starving artists, to be at long last bankable meant everything.

He said goodbye to Leslie. Maritza returned, cleared away his coffee cup and put a glass of water in his hand. He was no match for the women in his life today.

Sandro left the kitchen for the rooftop deck. Leslie's words echoed in his mind as he climbed the stairs. *You're home.* In recent years, he'd felt most at home on a movie set. That left him feeling adrift when he wasn't at work. Nothing balanced about that.

He grabbed a net and scooped out a few leaves floating on the pool's surface. He hadn't come up here for pool maintenance. He needed a visual aid to relive last night.

May I touch you?

Please.

He stretched out on a lounge chair and finally replied to Gigi's message. He was all in. Except for the drinks at the museum part. They could count him out of that. He had something else in mind.

Meet up with you at Basel.

Six

Art Basel, Opening Night

For four days in December, Miami Beach was the epicenter of the art world. Art Basel drew a wealthy, well-heeled crowd with money to waste on or to invest in, depending on whom you asked, modern art. A convention center the size of a warehouse was divvied up into viewing rooms, similar to booths at any bazaar worth wandering in. Each exhibitor's room rivaled the other, some were stark and spare, others were kaleidoscopes of colors and light. But each showcased carefully curated collections from around the world. A Picasso, a Warhol, a Lichtenstein print, a bedazzled Buddha, a miniature porcelain toilet, or a bust of Columbus made entirely of chewing gum—it all counted as art. And Angel was here for it.

Too bad she was too distracted to appreciate it fully. With every blink of the eye, she was back in paradise, kissing Alessandro Cardenas under a waterfall. The memory was tangible; she could feel the water rush and swirl between her breasts and his hard body pressed against hers.

Angel massaged her temples in a fruitless effort to erase the memory. *Oh, God! Please. Let me forget.*

Her mental state wasn't lost on her boss. "Angel! You're as shaky as a Chihuahua! Please calm down."

Perfect! The night had not yet begun and Angel had managed to piss off Paloma. As the newest member of the Gallery Six team, she wasn't part of the elite sales force led by the flame-haired Paloma Gentry. Angel was meant to stay behind and man the Lincoln Road shop like a sad and sorry Cinderella while Paloma, Justine and the rest had twirled in the Basel spotlight. Justine's accident had thrown a wrench in that plan. Paloma (real name Paula) was so brittle, you'd think Angel had ordered the hit on her top salesperson. It was unfair. What had she done except be helpful? She'd successfully closed Justine's last deal, getting top dollar for the Juan David Valero painting. And here she was tonight, looking damn good in Miami's answer to Millennial Pink and glowing like never before. She'd gone the extra mile and added some temporary golden highlights to her wavy brown hair. Bottom line: she was ready.

Was she just going to gloss over the part where she had sex with the client straight after closing the sale? Yes, as sure as the sun set in the west.

Paloma clapped to get her attention. Wearing all black and a ton of gold jewelry, red hair pulled into a severe bun, she had gallerista style down pat. "We are competing with galleries from Europe and all over the world. We have to measure up. Celebrities can smell nervousness. It's a turnoff."

"We wouldn't want to do that."

"No, we wouldn't," Paloma said. "Listen. I know you're a bit rough around the edges. That's understandable. A degree in fine arts doesn't prepare you for the art world. But you're going to give me an ulcer if you don't calm down."

Angel took offense at that. Her edges were smooth as silk, thank you very much! Besides, this wasn't her first Basel. It was her second. Her first visit to the art show dated back to when she qualified for a student discount, but still.

"Go and grab a drink at the lounge before the night gets going and the A-listers show up."

According to Paloma, there was Europe and the rest of the world, A-listers and ordinary people who weren't worth her time. But for all of her poise and polish, Paloma came undone when any B-lister wandered into their gallery.

She had almost made it to the exhibitors' lounge when it struck her: one of those highly anticipated A-listers could very well be Alessandro. She'd sort of ruled that out, since he'd had his art home delivered and all. But he was in town for Art Basel and this was the premier event. Why wouldn't he swing by with his colorful friends?

Angel dashed over to the bar for that drink she now sorely needed. The bartender gave her a choice of red, white or rosé. She picked the latter—strong enough to mend her nerves, but too light to mess with her head. Despite everything, Angel had to perform tonight. She had a job to do, a boss to impress and a commission to earn. The extra earnings would go a long way to help her relocate back home to Orlando.

Whenever Angel got to this point of her loosely strung plan, she felt a strange pang in her chest. Why was she having second thoughts about moving? Miami was an expensive city and with such stiff competition, she'd likely never get ahead here. She wouldn't miss the gallery. She would, however, miss Miami and its thriving art scene. Only this city wasn't her home and had never been her dream until Chris sold her on it. For that reason, and that reason only, she wanted a fresh start. She needed one.

A man approached the bar and, of the choices of red, white and rosé, opted for Patrón. There was nothing earth-shattering about that except for the man's deep, rich voice. Angel shivered. It couldn't be. She risked a sideways glance and found herself staring into a pair of dark eyes set in a face so ruggedly handsome it made her want to laugh and cry at the same time.

"Hello, Angel."

She died.

The last time she'd seen him looking this good, he was lording over her from a billboard, sporting a Rolex and a smile, while she stewed in traffic on I-95. Last night, at home in damp swim shorts and a crumpled shirt, he was amiable and approachable. She'd come close to forgetting his celebrity status so many times. Tonight, in what looked like a Tom Ford charcoal gray suit, clean-shaven, clear-eyed, he was killing her. Since she was hyperventilating, she had no choice but to accept that she was fangirling… hard. So much so that when the bartender placed her glass before her, she promptly knocked it over.

"Dammit!"

Alessandro closed the gap between them. "Are you okay?"

Her primary concern was for her dress. It was a Cush-nie classic, rented from a designer clothing website. As she frantically brushed away the few drops that had splashed onto the silk-draped bodice, she spit out a jumble of words. "Yes. Sure. I'm fine. Yup."

Oh, joy! One look into his eyes and she'd suffered a mini-stroke. She might as well admit it: Paloma was right.

She was a nervous wreck, shakier than a Chihuahua, not quite ready for primetime, golden highlights and all.

He handed her a cocktail napkin. "Here you go."

She wanted to thank him; instead, she reprimanded him. "What are you doing here?"

A slow smile crept to his lips. "Drowning my sorrows in tequila."

She doubted that very much. "The VIP lounge is down that way."

"Can't I hang out here?" he asked, lips twitching with that smile. "I promise I won't cause trouble."

Angel stared at him. She'd kissed those lips. She'd done more than that, but that was as far back as her mind would safely take her. "Obviously, I can't chase you away."

"True," he said. "But you could always run. Again."

"I didn't run..." Angel's voice sounded foreign to her own ears, so she thought it best to shut up.

The bartender who'd been minding his own business until now rushed forward. "Mr. Cardenas! You are welcome here, sir!"

Alessandro brought a finger to his lips. "Keep it quiet. I'm flying under the radar."

Now that was a waste of time. A star-studded international art fair was not the place to go incognito. Besides, any radar sweeping the area tonight would gravitate to him. Who was he wearing? What was he buying? Who was he taking home? Et cetera.

"I didn't mean to make you feel unwelcome," Angel said, mainly to appease the bartender. "Just wanted to point out that there's a full bar in the VIP."

He didn't have to settle for red, white or rosé when the exclusive collectors' lounge was top shelf only.

The bartender wouldn't hear it. "Never mind that. We

can get you anything you want. Patrón Platinum, of course. We have an excellent limited edition—"

"Silver is fine," Alessandro said. "On ice." Then he turned to Angel. "What were you drinking?"

"The young lady was enjoying a rosé," the bartender replied on her behalf.

"Not sure she got a chance to enjoy it."

The mess on the counter was wiped away and a fresh glass, poured from a far superior bottle, was set before her. The drinks were free. Alessandro slipped a fifty-dollar bill across the counter and the grateful bartender took the tip—and the hint—and backed away.

"Missed you this morning," he said. "Missed me?"

Angel let out a shaky breath. Why did she like him so much? "Listen, I didn't run out on you. I was late for work and…you were sleeping and… I didn't want to wake you and…that's all."

"That doesn't answer my question."

Two women sporting matching silver bobs and chatting excitedly approached the bar.

"I do want to highlight the pieces from our new artist," one said. "That should be our focus. What do you think?"

The other woman stared blankly. "I, uh… Sandro?"

Ah! Poor thing! She'd gone brain dead. Angel knew the signs.

He said hello and the women swooned. Angel took Alessandro by the elbow and steered him to a cocktail table.

"How did you find me?" she asked. She thought she might bump into him before the end of the night, but this felt targeted.

"I'm here to meet friends," he said. "I took a wrong turn somewhere and ended up at the wrong bar—and there you were."

He hadn't been looking for her, after all. Her "check ego" dashboard light flashed red. "I'm glad we ran into each other. I meant to apologize for the way I left."

It was a big fat lie, necessary only to salvage her pride. If he could act cool and collected, so could she.

He picked up his glass and gave the ice a rattle. "Whatever you say."

Angel watched him over the rim of her glass. He hadn't bought a word she'd said. "Okay. I left the way I did because I didn't want to drag things out," she said. "I know the rules."

"What rules?" he asked. "There are none."

It was highly possible that in Alessandro Cardenas's happy-go-lucky world there were no preset rules. He did as he pleased.

"The rules of the one-night stand," she explained.

He sipped his tequila slowly. "I'm trying to remember the last time I had one of those. It's been a while. Generally, my lovers want to keep me around."

Angel went very still, his words painting visions in her mind. His lovers were braver souls than she'd ever be. Although she hated the cowardly way she'd ducked out this morning, she did not regret much else. This was not a game she could play, not anymore. She was happiest and most secure when in a stable relationship, which meant she tended to keep random boyfriends long past their expiration dates. It also meant that she tended to choose partners with an eye for long-term compatibility. That simply wasn't the case here. Even so, she couldn't let him score this point.

"My lovers have never complained," she said.

This was true. If there were a Good Housekeeping Seal of Approval on keeping a lover happy, even if just temporarily, she would have earned it. And so would he. He'd left her blissed out. Which raised the question: Had she seriously cheated herself out of early morning sex for the sake of keeping her emotions neat and tidy?

He leaned close and whispered, "I believe it, Angel."

With him so close, she yearned to touch his face, to feel the smooth skin that was rugged the night before. She wanted him to kiss her neck again, to turn back time and relive it all, to have him take her home.

"Alessandro, I have to go…" she said plaintively. "I've got to get back to work before I get in trouble."

"What kind of trouble?"

"The kind you get into when your boss gives you a five-minute break and you hang out at the bar with your ex-lover for about a half hour!"

"I'm your ex?" he said, indignant. "After just one night?"

Angel dropped her hands onto the tabletop in despair and almost knocked her glass over again. Good thing it was empty. "It is what it is. Now I have to go."

Alessandro drained his glass then stood up straight and tugged at the cuffs of his shirt. "Okay. Let's go."

"Where are you going?" she asked.

"I got you in trouble. I'm getting you out of it."

She started to back away. "How?"

"I have my ways."

"Are you nuts? My boss can't know!" she protested, on the edge of panic.

The wicked grin came out to play. "Know about what, Angel?"

She glared at him. Was it too late to ask him to stop calling her by her nickname? Angeline was her grandmother's name and her world wouldn't stop spinning if he called her that.

"I can be discrete," he said. "Can you?"

Angel pinched the bridge of her nose. Which god had she angered to deserve this?

"Do you want my help or not?" he said.

She looked him in the eye, prepared to turn him down. He shoved his hands in his pockets and waited for an answer. The gesture caused his unbuttoned shirt collar to split and reveal the dip in his brown throat. She faltered. Why lie? She wanted it oh so very much.

Seven

Paloma was darting around their booth like a goldfish in a bag of water. When Angel approached, she snapped. "Where were you?" Then she got a glimpse of her companion and went pale everywhere except her cheeks that remained orgasm pink, courtesy of NARS Cosmetics.

"Look who I ran into," Angel said innocently.

"Sorry if I've kept Angeline away too long," Alessandro said. "I've been to this circus so many times, you'd think I'd know my way around. She was a big help."

Paloma rushed forward. "The convention center is a madhouse maze. Good thing Angel is resourceful."

Angel sighed with relief. No one short of an A-lister could have saved her from Paloma's wrath.

"I'm Paloma Gentry. How may *I* help you?"

Alessandro's response was polite but firm. "I'm with Angeline. Thank you."

Paloma looked as if she had to gulp for air. "I'll leave you to it."

Paloma went to her minidesk, set up like a throne in a corner of their viewing room. If a side-eye could kill, Angel would have had a gash across her throat.

She turned to Alessandro. "Thanks for using your influence to aid and assist the underprivileged."

"You're welcome, Angeline," he said. "I do what I can."

She had to stop flip-flopping on this, but she wished he'd quit calling her Angeline. He was doing it deliberately, to put distance between them, and all of a sudden she didn't like it.

"Alright," he said. "I think you're in the clear.

Show me what you've got."

A personal challenge lurked in his words, and she took it up. Angel looked around and picked a piece at random. Their collection was a little mix of everything, curated to draw in the social media crowd. Their featured pieces made for good Instagram content, but there were some hidden gems as well.

Angel led him straight to the crowd pleasers: neon text art with catchy phrases. "Here we have *YOLO*, by a young local artist." She pointed to the bold yellow letters with the poise of Vanna White.

Alessandro was nodding, as if YOLO were gospel. "I've got that tattooed somewhere."

She stifled a laugh. "No, you don't."

He slid her a glance. "How would you know?"

Heat rushed to her cheeks. Now she was turning orgasm pink. "I can't get into it right now."

"Want to get into it later?"

His gaze stayed on her, holding her in place—otherwise, she would have gone to pieces. "I'm working."

He pointed to the large yellow letters. "You only live once, Angel. What time do you get off work?"

"This thing ends at midnight," she said, before she could think better of it. She did not want to encourage him. "Let's continue."

Angel hurried along with the tour. She showed him an acrylic on canvas painting of a lemon and a lime, titled *Lemon Lime,* a collage of a bull dog, titled *Bruce*, and a flashing neon sign with the words: *Sorry. It's Me, Not You.*

He paused at that one. "The last time I used that excuse it didn't go so well."

"Bad breakup?" she asked.

"Is there any other kind?"

For once, Angel didn't spiral backward into a whirlpool of her tragic memories. Instead, she flipped through a mental catalogue of the gorgeous actresses and models that Alessandro had been photographed with over the years. Something inside her shrank. Under ordinary circumstances her self-esteem was rock solid, but nothing was ordinary about this.

"May I ask you a question?" she said.

"You can ask me anything."

Paloma chose that moment to return with champagne. "Mr. Cardenas, for you!"

Only a flicker of his lashes betrayed any trace of impatience, and Angel was sure Paloma had missed it. He accepted the flute of Veuve Clicquot, thanked her and dispatched her with a nod. He did not drink from the glass, but he used it to point at her. "You were saying."

Angel took a breath. She was just going to come out with it, before Paloma swung back around with an offering of pigs in a blanket or whatever. Who knew when they would speak again? "Please, don't get me wrong."

"I'll try not to."

"What do you want with me? There are so many more... fascinating women here."

Alessandro studied her a while before turning his attention to a glass sculpture of a dolphin. "You know what I was doing six years ago?"

"I don't."

"Serving drinks to fascinating women."

"You were a bartender?" Could he mix a decent margarita? Not too sour. Not too sweet?

"I was a bartender and a waiter and everything you can think of," he said. "These fascinating women were not interested in struggling waiters/actors."

"You're not struggling anymore." Angel felt the need to point this out in case he hadn't gotten the memo. Maybe his accountant had failed to inform him, but his net worth was up there.

He ran a thumb along the smooth curved lines of the sculpture. She wished he wouldn't touch the art, particularly because it reminded her of the way he had touched her.

"Here's something that might interest you." She led him to the opposing wall, where a series of black-and-white photographs, titled *Devastation*, were on display. The series featured photos of Haiti after the 2010 earthquake, Bahamas after Hurricane Dorian, and Puerto Rico after the island was hit last summer by both varieties of natural disasters. "These photographs cut to the heart of the climate crisis by laying bare the consequences."

Alessandro studied each print. "I'm interested."

"Oh? You have the option of acquiring the complete series or just one or two pieces. It's up to you."

"The series is not complete," he said.

"What do you mean?"

"Where is Cuba after Hurricane Irma?"

He was Cuban. The missing photograph must be jarring to him. "Arranging last-minute travel to Cuba is difficult, particularly after a disaster."

"Difficult, not impossible."

Wonderful! She'd managed to insult her ex-lover with her activist art.

"I'll take it," he said, surprising her. "The whole thing."

"Don't you want to know how much it costs?"

"I'm sure you'll tell me."

"Each original photograph is nine thousand dollars."

"Sold."

The words she uttered next made no sense. "You don't have to do that."

"Why not?" he said.

She looked around to make sure Paloma wasn't within earshot. "If you're doing this to help me, you've done enough. Just look at this crowd."

Their little viewing room was drawing people in and the object of their curiosity wasn't the art. Angel had noticed a few well-heeled attendees angling camera phones, sneaking photographs. So much for the 1 percent living above the fray!

"What makes you think I don't want it?"

His tone made her question what exactly he was talking about.

"I only meant, you don't have to pretend."

"Pretend to want the things I want."

They were in their own private bubble now. The growing crowd fading to nothing.

"You should be sure…" She hesitated. "Before mistakes are made. It's a substantial investment."

"It's good work and I have plans for it."

"In that case, I'll ring you up."

"Angel," he said, stopping her before she could turn

away. "You fascinate me. And I don't think this is a mistake."

Stunned, Angel picked a distant point to stare at. Unfortunately, the point was part of a gigantic mobile and now her whole world was spinning.

"I get that you don't want things to get messy, and I can't promise you that they won't. Given the chance, wouldn't you want to make a mess with me?"

Paloma, proving that she could be counted on to kill anyone's joy, returned, this time with an offer. "By any chance, Mr. Cardenas, are you interested in acquiring any more of your grandfather's artwork? We were delighted that Angel was able to finalize the sale in Justine's absence. But Justine is just a phone call away."

Excuse me? What? His grandfather?

Paloma likely did not miss Angel's confounded expression, nor did she miss the opportunity to school Angel in front of a client. "Juan David Valero is Mr. Cardenas's grandfather."

"I see." Why was she only learning this now? Why hadn't Justine given her the heads-up? Or Paloma included that nugget in the prepared statement she had texted her? And for the love of God, why hadn't Alessandro *told* her?

"If you are interested, just let me know. We don't come across a Valero too often—that's safe to say. Still, Justine could make some inquiries. Are you interested?"

"I am." Alessandro handed her a card. The way she beamed at it, you would have thought he had handed her the winning Powerball numbers. "If you find anything, get back to me."

"Sandro! Finally! There you are!"

Angel turned in time to catch the green-eyed brunette elbowing her way through the crowd. Wearing Chanel from head to toe, she looked...rich. Her face was expertly painted with shadows and highlights accentuating her delicate features.

"Gigi," Alessandro said with zero enthusiasm. "You've found me."

Gigi pulled out her phone and placed a call, canceling a search party. "I got him. Meet you at the entrance in five."

"You make it sound like I'm a fugitive," Alessandro said.

"We had to split up to look for you," she said reproachfully. "You weren't answering your phone."

"Sorry. It's off."

"You're not buying more art, are you?"

"I am."

"You are?" This was news to Paloma.

"Yes," Angel said, her voice shaky. "Mr. Cardenas is interested in *Devastation*."

"What's that?" Gigi asked.

"A photography series," Paloma informed her.

"Oh, good. So long as it's not that stupid banana taped to the wall." She tapped Alessandro's arm in a chummy way. "Have you seen it?"

"Nope," Alessandro said. "You've seen one, you've seen them all."

Everyone laughed except for Angel. She did not find him funny, not when he'd withheld information that was pertinent to her job. It explained so much. His blatant disinterest. His insistence that he was "familiar" with the painting. He could have expounded on that.

He was looking at her, his expression contrite. "Angeline, should we finalize the sale?"

"No need!" Paloma chimed. "We have your information and we can handle things on our end. I will send you an electronic invoice. Once settled, we'll have the photographs shipped to your home address."

"That was painless!" Gigi exclaimed. "Now let's get out of here before you buy anything else. We're late for dinner."

Alessandro rested his eyes on Angel, his gaze soft.

She pasted a smile on her face. "Thanks for your business, Mr. Cardenas! Always a *pleasure*."

She couldn't help but torture him a little. Unfortunately, she'd drawn the attention of his friend. She focused on Angel as if seeing her for the first time. Then her lips curled up in the faintest smile. "Hi," she said. "I'm Georgina."

Fascinating women... "I'm Angeline."

"Nice to meet you," she said. "I'm Sandro's friend. We're just friends. We go way back."

Alessandro looked up and away. "I think she got your point."

"Just making sure," she said. "Now I hate to do this, but we really have to go. We've got reservations. Friends are waiting."

Alessandro sought her eyes as if to communicate a quiet apology. Angel stiffened and looked down at her hands. Then Gigi tugged at his arm and led him away, all the while cooing, *"I approve! She's beautiful!"*

Paloma rushed off to finalize the sale. If she'd picked up on anything, she didn't seem to care. Only Angel stood bolted in place. She watched Alessandro go and didn't turn away until he vanished into the crowd, until he was lost to her.

Eight

The six of them were seated in a private dining room at a round table beneath a massive chandelier. The lights were dim enough to hide Sandro's discomfort. His friends were roasting him tonight.

"I caught the vibe between them within a nanosecond," Gigi said. "And he was so shy around her. It was *adorable*!"

Sandro had never been shy a day of his life. But by the time Gigi had come around, he'd been actively avoiding Angel's gaze. The revelation about his grandfather had not gone over well.

"We met her last night," Jenny Xi said. "It was riveting to watch."

"They were on fire," Jordan said.

"I liked her," Rose said. "Why didn't she join us?"

"She's working tonight," Sandro said.

"Ah! La pauvre!" Rose lamented.

"Pobrecita!" Rolando Ramirez echoed in Spanish. He was the front man of a local band that had just picked up its first Latin Grammy. Sandro, Jordan and Rolando had attended the same high school for the performing arts and, by all accounts, were doing pretty well.

"Don't feel sorry for her," Gigi said. "Apparently, she's very good at her job. She sold Romeo here a series of photographs at ten grand a pop."

"Nine grand," Sandro corrected. "And it's for the cause. I'll be auctioning them off tomorrow."

"That's so good of you!" Gigi cried. "Tell me again. Why aren't we a couple?"

"Back off," Jenny Xi said sternly. "I'm Team Angeline."

"So am I," Rose said. *"Absolument."*

"Me, too!" Rolando said. "And I've never met the woman. But I'm married and I want you guys to catch up."

"Sorry to disappoint you all, but she wants nothing to do with me."

"A woman turned you down?" Jenny looked doubtful. "Hard to believe."

"I promise you it's happened before," Sandro said, putting a playful spin on a painful subject. "Gigi, will you have me?"

"No, thanks. I'm Team Angeline, too." She raised her wineglass. "And I'm all for raising money at auction. For the cause!"

"For the cause!" they cheered.

Gigi's father was a famous baseball star, but he'd made his fortune off the diamond by investing in Florida real estate. Her mother had organized tomorrow's fundraising auction. It was a ploy to draw attention to her newly renovated Miami Beach hotel. Sandro didn't mind playing along for a good cause. His contribution was a mere drop of rain in the ocean. The press made a fuss about it when, really, he was doing the bare minimum. This was the only part of fame that truly bothered him. Acclaim, adulation, loss of privacy—all things he'd prepared himself for. This was the life he'd wanted and he had zero qualms about it. But when they put him on a pedestal like some kind of benevolent god, he made sure to set the record straight. A flawed man, he'd let people down, broken hearts, and was known to hold a grudge. He wanted the public to celebrate his work, not to conflate him with the heroes he portrayed.

He'd complained once to Gigi and she put it all in perspective. "In five to seven years' time, when you're teetering on forty, no one will give a damn what you do. So hang in there, buddy. This too shall pass."

She was right. Only well-respected veteran actors got the opportunity to age in the business, snapping up the few good roles available. Sandro wanted a long career and to work in the industry for as many years as he'd waited tables and mixed drinks until 2:00 a.m. These were the years and he had to make them count. That left little time for relationships. He wasn't even thinking about marriage. Oddly, that thought brought him back to Angeline.

She had a sensitive heart, which she could not hide— not from him, anyway. Her emotions pooled in her eyes. For that reason, guilt and regret churned in his gut all evening. Sandro hadn't missed her hurt expression when the gallery manager brought up his grandfather. At the time he could not pause to explain, not with the manager dangling red meat before him. She could find him more paintings. Wasn't that interesting? And then Gigi had arrived.

"It's bad luck not to toast," Rose scolded him.

Sandro looked around the table. His friends were holding up their cocktail glasses, all waiting on him. So he raised his glass to the cause. When Gigi went on to discuss their plans for the rest of the night, Sandro tuned her out.

He had to get to Angel. He owed her an apology.

His angel was blond tonight, a detail that he had somehow missed earlier. Standing in the light of the streetlamps, newly added golden strands shimmered down the length of her wavy hair. The December night air had a bite to it. She tightened the belt of her white trench coat. All around her, people were chatting and laughing. She looked serious, brows drawn as she studied her phone. Was she still receiving alerts on her ex? It was her prerogative. Rebound sex wasn't magic. So why the pang of jealousy? When she looked up from her phone, she looked lost and, frankly, sad. Whoever had caused her to feel that way could die a slow and painful death.

If only he didn't have a sneaking suspicion that he was the one to blame.

He got out of his borrowed car and leaned against the door. He was double-parked and blocking the flow of traffic. The only reason the crossing guard wasn't having a fit was because the Bentley was a beauty. The guard might not know who Sandro was, but he knew that he was *someone*. Sandro had always hated guys who pulled stunts like this, and yet here he was.

The event had wrapped up a while ago, but chaos outside the convention center had not died down. Angeline stood apart from the crowd, staring straight ahead. She had a way of folding within herself. Earlier, when he'd spotted her at the bar, she'd had that same unsearchable look on her face.

Then suddenly her gaze sharpened with recognition. "Alessandro!"

She shouted his name, drawing the attention of a few

people. He didn't care. He was transfixed with the woman making her way toward him, her eyes brilliant with anger and her hair, caught in the night breeze, flapping around her face.

"What are you doing out here blocking traffic?"

She was so practical. It was adorable. "I was hoping for a chance to speak with you."

Going by her body language alone, he expected her to say, "Get lost. I never want to see you again." Instead she said, "My Uber canceled, I need a ride home."

Sandro held open the car door. "Get in before they tow me away." She glared at him again before climbing into the back seat. He got behind the wheel just in time to hear her sigh with relief. In the rearview mirror, he watched as she got settled.

"Did you have a good night?" he asked.

She fastened her seatbelt with a snap. "I had a long night."

"Where do you live?"

"Key Biscayne."

"That far?"

"Is that a problem?"

"It's a long commute for you. That's all I meant to say." He put the car in gear. "Do you have a car?"

"I do," she said. "It's been leaking oil and I don't have time to get it repaired this week."

He could offer to have it repaired or he could offer to drive her around this week. He was tossing around these options in his head when she leaned forward and proceeded to give him instructions. "Make a right at the light and head to West 41st Street."

"If I needed directions, Siri, I would have asked."

She let out an exasperated gasp, implying that he was behaving like a typical man.

"Before I worked my way up to bartending, I delivered takeout," he explained. "I know this area like the back of my hand."

"Okay, fine," she said. "But every other week a road closes and the map changes."

Good point.

"You don't have to keep doing this," she added.

"What?"

"Spinning the tale of your humble roots," she replied. "It's as if you want to prove that you're an ordinary guy, all the while driving a car that costs more than a house. It's jarring."

Another good point. Although, he hadn't been aware that that was what he was doing. He wanted her to like him, to trust him. Was that wrong?

"This car belongs to Georgina's mother," he said.

"Relatable," she said. "Last week I borrowed my neighbor's scooter so I could run an errand."

Traffic was crawling at a snail's pace, which explained why her ride might've canceled. As they sat in the dark, motionless car, silence took over. He chanced a glance at the rearview mirror and their eyes met.

"Hi, Angel."

She did not blink. "You lied to me."

"I withheld information," he said. "That's not the same."

"You let me make a fool of myself, rattling on about your grandfather's nostalgia." She turned to the window with a huff. "You must have thought I was an idiot."

Humiliation rang through her voice. A half-assed apology wasn't going to cut it.

"I'm sorry," he said.

She did not respond. Sandro stared at her until the blare of car horns jolted him into action. The light had long turned green and the drivers behind him were impatient.

He focused on his driving, checking on her from time to time. Her body language was not encouraging. She sat with her arms folded across her chest, the collar of her light trench coat—her only nod to winter—drawn close to her throat. He waited until they were cruising on the highway before he spoke again.

"Why do you think you never heard that Juan David Valero was my grandfather?"

"Because I'm a novice who didn't prepare?"

"Because I've kept it hidden for the most part."

She leaned forward and gripped his headrest. "Then how did Paloma know? I'm sure Justine knew!"

He had no clue. And yet Paloma's sudden expertise on all things JD was suspicious. "My grandfather, the great painter, died penniless. But he left me his greatest treasure."

"His art?" She was still gripping his headrest, but her voice was less harsh.

"That's right."

She fell back against the seat. "Oh… I thought…"

"You thought what?"

"Nothing."

She was not getting away with that. He'd shared something personal. She could reciprocate a little. "Tell me."

"I thought you didn't care about art."

"What made you think that?" he said.

"Last night you barely looked at the painting."

"Now you know why," Sandro said. "I was familiar with it, just like I said. And you could've given me the benefit of the doubt. I traveled across the country for an art show."

"That means nothing."

Yet another fair point. The city was crawling with celebrities, none of which were even remotely interested in art. Most would spend their days on the beach and nights at the clubs. But most people knew where he stood.

"Angel, I come from a long line of artists, going back generations. They were not famous and they didn't win awards. They were dedicated and serious." Before she could say anything, he added, "That's not another anecdote to make me relatable. It's the truth of who I am."

She did not say much the rest of the way. Gradually, the tension drained from the car. He felt comfortable with her. It had been this way since, well, yesterday.

"Head onto Rickenbacker, then a left on Galen Drive."

Sandro followed her directions without objection, sailing over the bridge that arched over the dark bay. Was he disappointed that the long drive had turned out to be not all that long? Yeah, particularly because he was certain Angel would not invite him up.

She lived in a rental community named Coral Rock. She used a clicker to raise the gate arm and pointed to the nearest available parking spot in the large flat lot. As expected, she thanked him for the ride and reached for the car door handle.

"Angel..."

She silenced him. "It's pointless, Alessandro. You and I...we orbit around different suns."

"Why is that a problem?" he asked, arguing even though he knew that letting her go was the best thing to do.

She reached forward again. This time, she lightly raked her fingertips through his hair. Sandro shivered at her touch. He took hold of her hand and brought the palm to his lips. Her rose-scented perfume filled his nostrils.

"I'm glad you came by," she said. "Not because I needed a ride, although that helped. But I needed to make sense of what happened tonight. Thank you."

She gently freed her hands from his and slipped out of the car.

The five-story building was pistachio green. The apartment doors opened onto a breezeway corridor. Sandro watched as she climbed the stairs leading to the top floors and waited until a light came on in a third-floor apartment. *It's over.* Then he pulled out of the parking lot and drove into the night.

Nine

"Angel! What's the matter? Why are you hyperventilating?"

Angel was jogging along the bridge when her phone buzzed in her hand. It was Justine Carr. No matter the circumstances, she managed to spike every encounter with a bit of drama. Angel adjusted her earbuds. "I'm fine, Justine. Out for an early run, that's all."

After a fitful night, Angel had given up on sleep. She swapped her pajama shorts for running shorts and took off into the dawn. One of the perks of living in Key Biscayne was the scenic path over the bridge to the sandy beach that doubled as the neighborhood's dog park. A run had a way of clearing her head, something she desperately needed. He was haunting her. Last night she'd done the sensible thing and ended their affair—and even that was too strong of a word. It was a hookup gone awry, and not for the reasons she'd allowed him to believe.

He had been less than forthcoming about his grandfather, but she sort of understood why and had accepted his apology. What she could not get over, however, was her own treacherous heart. Standing on the curb last night, despairing that her ride had canceled due to overwhelming traffic, she'd looked up, seen him and instantly felt safe. He was here, and he'd take care of her.

What fresh batch of nonsense was that?

He was not the hero in her melodrama. She had no business feeling warm and gooey inside, no business hearing a choir of angels when he said something as simple as "Hi."

She had to get herself together and fast before she hopped onto the first ferry back to Fisher Island.

"Wish I could go for walks," Justine said wistfully.

Angel had forgotten that she was on a call. "How are you feeling?"

"Like an idiot, but I'll survive."

"Anything I can do for you?"

"You can attend tonight's event at The High Tide."

"Why do I have to go?" she whined. Great, she was a whiner now.

"Because I can't!"

"Why can't Paloma go? She's the manager."

"Paloma is pulling long shifts at the convention center. Then she's meeting with a private client. Besides, we need someone who'll stand out. Paloma is pretty much useless after ten p.m., or haven't you noticed?"

"I haven't, to be honest."

Justine let out a heavy sigh. Originally from Monroe County, she had the pronounced drawl of a kid who grew up in the Lower Keys. "This is Basel, the big time, and we all have to do our part. Paloma is running the show. I'm processing the orders from home. It's your job to go to the parties and represent us. We can't be absent from the scene. We expect you to take photos for our social media accounts. If you're smart, you'll make some contacts."

"Fine. I'll go."

"Quit moaning!" Justine said. "If I were your age and had your legs, I'd have the city at my feet. Don't forget to stop by the gallery to pick up the invitation, along with your commission."

"Commission for what?"

"The Cardenas deal," Justine replied. "You know what? I don't think fresh air is doing you much good."

It scandalized Angel that she should earn a commission for *all the things* that she had done. She might have to pass on that.

"Justine, did you know..."

"Know what?"

"Nothing. Never mind."

Angel ended the call. She walked along the bridge, stopping at the halfway point to watch the boats criss-crossing the bay. Even though she'd wanted answers, discussing Alessandro's private business seemed wrong. It didn't matter what Paloma and Justine knew or when they knew it. He was not comfortable with anyone knowing about his grandfather. If Angel owed him anything, it was discretion.

Sandro arrived at the Lincoln Road gallery shortly past seven. At this early hour, the open-air mall was deserted, except for a few joggers. The designer shops and restaurants were all closed, and so was Gallery Six. Paloma Gentry greeted him at the door.

"Thank you for accommodating me," Sandro said. He could not swing by during regular hours without drawing too much attention. Lincoln Road was nothing but a backdrop for people watching. He had to get out before the sidewalk traffic picked up and he was spotted, photographed, hounded. And lately, if he patronized a business, even if just to pick up a pack of gum or beer, it was perceived as an endorsement. Since he would rather not endorse Gallery Six, discretion was in order. He could have sent a proxy, but he felt as if he owed it to his grandfather to handle this himself.

"It's no trouble," she said. "I live above the gallery."

She locked the glass door behind him.

Gallery Six was smaller than he had imagined. They'd made the most of the viewing space— paintings cluttered the walls and the floor was dotted with sculptures and art objects displayed on pedestals. At the register was the usual assortment of postcards and Miami Beach souvenirs. He found himself wondering where Angeline Louis fit into all this.

Paloma invited him to her office and offered him coffee or tea. He wasn't going to make a social call out of this. "No, thank you."

"Very well." She opened what looked like a filing cabinet and pulled out a small painting, no bigger than an iPad. His grandfather liked to paint on a large scale. This seemingly endless parade of miniatures was grating on him.

"This is *La Playa*."

Alessandro took the canvas from Paloma. It was, as its name suggested, a rendering of a beach in thick swirls of oil paint. The sky was a hazy blue gray, and in the foreground the waves thinned and spread onto pale blond sand. Seagulls, a lone palm tree and a little boy taking a nap, completed the composition. It was a signature Juan David Valero piece.

Although his grandfather never regretted fleeing Communist Cuba, he spent his entire adult life longing for the idyllic settings of his childhood. But something was off about this painting. The small size was only part of it. It didn't move him like his grandfather's other paintings never failed to do. It didn't bring back his grandfather's voice, his paint-stained hands or the smell of turpentine that clung to his clothes. That wouldn't make sense to anyone else. It was part of the bond that they'd shared and, he knew now, his father and half brother had envied.

"You say my grandfather painted this, but I've never seen it, or even sketches of it."

"That's not unusual. It dates back to before you were born."

"Where did you get it from?" he asked.

"A private collector who prefers to remain anonymous."

Paloma backed away from him and went to stand behind her desk. Her auburn hair was the color of autumn and she wore it in a tight bun at the base of her neck. Her eyes were a watery blue.

"That's convenient."

"Selling off art is like pawning the family jewels. It's unseemly and you wouldn't want your friends to know. Our clients can count on our discretion." She flashed a toothy, shark-like grin. "Trust me. It's best for everyone involved. I can answer any questions you may have. You have concerns about the provenance of this piece?"

"I do."

"Alright." Paloma let out the weary sigh of the expert having to explain basics to the novice. "We work with industry experts. Every piece comes with a certificate of authenticity."

The certificate was BS, and she knew it. A painting wasn't a designer purse.

"Is the seller in financial trouble?" Sandro asked. He was just fishing around here. Paloma was a stone-cold professional. There was no getting water from rock.

"Why does it matter? Are you worried the seller didn't value your grandfather's work?"

No one would value his grandfather's work as much as he did. His interest had to do with his aversion to being duped. But he'd gone far enough with this. He wished he could walk out and leave the painting on her desk, but he couldn't do it. Fake or not, *La Playa* belonged to him.

"How much?"

She looked him dead in the eye. "Thirty-five thousand."

Sandro didn't flinch. "Ring me up."

The High Tide was high glamour. Angel opted for a slinky LBD, a little *blue* dress. The dress was basically a variation of the pink one she'd worn the night before; only this one was a thrift shop find. She finished off the look with a swipe of red lipstick and heels. Faking confidence was an art form.

In the elevator taking her to the hotel's rooftop deck, Angel mapped out a strategy. She decided to ignore Justine's advice. What was the point of networking? She didn't know anyone, and no one gave a damn about her. She'd snap photos for the gallery's social media accounts, maybe even a livestream, and then she'd call it a night.

When the elevator doors slid open, she stepped into a wondrous world. Angel followed the other guests through a forest of papier-mâché palm trees, past a waterfall cascading into a white marble basin and around the pool-turned–dance floor until she found the bar. After quickly perusing the cocktail menu, she ordered a lychee martini. While she waited, she cast a look around at the moveable feast of ridiculously attractive people, not the least of which was the bartender. She recognized actors, models and opera singers. She spotted Julian and Nina Knight of Knight Films, a Miami power couple, holding court by the fountain. When her phone buzzed in her purse, Angel was grateful to have a genuine reason to stare at her phone—anything to keep from gawking.

Justine had sent her a text message:

BIG NEWS! AC is auctioning off Devastation tonight. Make sure you take photos so we can remind everyone where he got it!!!

AC? It took a minute for her brain to make the connection, but once it did, Angel shoved her phone in her purse as if it were radioactive. The part of her that had chosen to wear the dress, the sexy heels and the Fenty by Rihanna red lipstick had known there was a chance he'd be here tonight. It was one thing to suspect. It was another thing to receive written confirmation.

The bartender placed a decadent cocktail before her. "Here you go, gorgeous."

Bless his heart. She tipped him well.

Angel scanned the crowd. If she had eyes on him, she could stay out of his way. She'd hide behind a papier-mâché palm tree if need be. Then she'd take the photos and tiptoe out before he ever knew she was here. That was the plan.

"ANGELINE! Guys, look who's here!"

Angel closed her eyes and kissed her plan goodbye. Suddenly, she was pulled into a group hug with Jenny Xi, Rose Rachid and Georgina Garcia, air kisses all around.

"What are you doing here alone, *ma chérie*?" Rose asked. "Where is Alessandro?"

"I'm working tonight," Angel said, setting the record straight while trying to sound as cool as these women looked.

"You're always working!" Georgina said disapprovingly.

The woman was wearing this season's Dior pantsuit. Maybe, for her, work was voluntary rather than a mandatory activity.

"Put your Blackberry away," Jenny said. "Your squad is here!"

"What are you drinking?" Rose asked. "It looks delicious."

"A lychee martini."

"And that's what I'm having," Jenny said. She took Rose's hand. "We'll be at the bar."

Angel was left alone with Georgina in Dior, who was now demanding Angel call her "Gigi."

"Okay, Gigi," Angel said tentatively. "Where's Jordan tonight?"

"He's playing a set at The Zoo," she said. "We'll meet up with him later. But forget Jordan. I want to talk about Alessandro."

And I don't. Wasn't the whole point of small talk to avoid hot-button topics?

"He's here, you know. I'll give him a call, if you like."

"Don't bother!" Angel practically shouted the words. "I'm here for work. Remember?"

Gigi tossed a lock of caramel brown hair over her shoulder. Angel had never seen anyone so impeccably groomed, not up close anyway. Whoever did her highlights was a skilled artist.

"About Alessandro," she said. "He and I have some history."

Angel's throat tightened in the way it had when she'd watched Gigi and Alessandro walk away together last night. Soon, she'd be gasping for air.

"I was into him, and he didn't feel the same," Gigi said. "That's our history. The end."

That could mean any number of things. When had she figured out he wasn't into her? Had they been dating awhile?

"He starred in one of the first movies I produced."

"*Downward Spiral*."

"You've seen it?"

"It's one of my favorite films."

Gigi seemed genuinely pleased. "Thank you! It's a classic immigrant story. That's why I found it so compelling."

"Alessandro is great in it."

"He's great in everything," Gigi said matter-of-factly. "He's very serious about his career. Our working relationship was important to him. So I asked myself, was it worth it to muddy those waters? The answer was no, and I don't regret it. We're the best of friends *and* we have a great working relationship. I'm very lucky."

Lucky didn't scratch the surface. She was fortunate, privileged and clearly had the sort of upbringing that gave her the confidence to just speak her mind without fear of blowback.

"There's something else," she said.

Angel didn't want to know anything else, but that wasn't going to stop Gigi.

"He never looked at me the way he looked at you," she said.

"You're wrong," Angel said with a nervous hiccup of a laugh. "He didn't look at me in any particular way. A lot was going on last night and—"

"I'm not wrong," Gigi said flatly.

Angel took a long sip of her martini to hide her burning cheeks. Rose and Jenny returned with an extra cocktail for Gigi.

"The bartender is so hot, I almost climbed over the bar," Jenny said.

"She's not joking," Rose said. "I had to hold her back and remind her of our burning love."

Gigi tossed her head back and laughed. "Should we find out when he gets off work?"

A hush ran through the party crowd as musicians walked on the stage at the far end of the deck. After a quick sound test, the guitarist approached a microphone.

"That's Rolando!" Jenny whispered to Angel. The name didn't ring any bells...until it did. Rolando y Mafioso had had *the* hit song of the summer.

In a smooth baritone, Rolando said, "Ladies and gentlemen, beautiful people, give it up for my brother in the struggle, Alessandro Cardenas."

Alessandro joined the band on stage to thunderous applause. He held up a glass half-filled with amber liquor and ice, and saluted the audience.

The drummer got things going. "One! Two! One! Two! Three! Four!"

The band launched into a Buena Vista Social Club staple. Alessandro swayed with the tempo for a while. He approached the microphone, opened his mouth, and started to sing. His voice was raw honey.

Angel felt sure she was going to die.

"Oh, yeah," Gigi said. "Give him a fifth of rum and that happens."

Fingers curled around the stem of her glass, Angel tuned out everyone who was not Alessandro. Wearing black, like the rest of the band, his shirt was fitted and neatly tucked into his trousers, and yet he'd somehow neglected to fasten most of the buttons. He looked delicious. A golden spotlight added shimmer to his bronze skin. Eyes closed, brows drawn, he sang and seduced his audience.

The tempo picked up suddenly and one of the backup singers took off on a reggaeton tangent to the delight of the crowd. Then a trumpeter stepped forward for a solo that wrecked Angel's heart. All the while Sandro stood to the side, grooving in a world of his own. She focused on the way he moved, and remembered how they'd moved together. She'd done everything to squeeze that memory into a small space and lock it away. Now she wondered why she had ever wanted to.

Gigi approached again. "I never looked at him the way you do, so maybe that was my mistake."

Angel swiveled around to confront her, only to find Gigi, Jenny and Rose smiling at her without malice. They were harmless. She was ready to drop the act. Besides, Alessandro had returned to the microphone and let out a low, plaintive sound. His voice was smooth, but it also had grit. It wrapped around her, tugging her to him. Angel handed Gigi her cocktail glass. She moved toward the stage, angling her way through the crowd and leaving her newly acquired squad behind. She was vaguely aware of shouts and high fives. She heard Gigi pronounce triumphantly: "My job is done!" But nothing could tamper with the immediacy of Alessandro's voice.

Angel crossed the covered pool and with each step she had the sensation of walking on water. The instant he spotted her, his onyx eyes turned glossy. With the very next step she was walking on air.

The way he looked at her!

When she reached the stage, Alessandro neared the edge and hunched low. The sleeves of his shirt were rolled up to the elbows. All she'd have to do was reach out to feel his warm skin. How she'd held back from doing so was anyone's guess. He sang the last lyrics of the song just for her. The full meaning of the Spanish words escaped her, but she understood the longing they conveyed.

Life may have given Gigi the option to muddy the proverbial waters—Angel had no choice. She was neck deep in mud, and drowning fast.

Ten

Tonight, his angel was a devil in a blue dress.

Once the music died, Sandro tossed his microphone to Rolando and leaped off the stage. This impromptu jam session had taken him back to their high school days and he'd enjoyed it. The payoff, however, was greater than he could have ever hoped. If he believed in miracles, this would count as one. He was sure he'd blown it with Angel. He'd been pouring out his heartache on stage when she cut through the crowd. It was like a scene from a god-damn movie.

How would the night end?

The applause was thick and a small mob pushed toward the stage and gathered around him. Angel was cast aside in the melee. Sandro reached out and took hold of her hand before she slipped away. The band launched into one of their latest hits and his newly acquired fans dispersed.

Sandro gently pulled her to him and pressed a kiss to her temple. "Want to dance?"

She nodded and they took off with a whirl, as much as space permitted on the crowded dance floor. His moves were less than smooth. He was nervous and his joints were stiff. Plus the effort he put into holding her at an appropriate distance was going to kill him. But that lasted only until another couple bumped into them, pushing Angel into his arms. He tightened his grip on her waist to steady her and, once he had her in his arms, he could not let go. She pressed her forehead to his chin and her breath fanned his throat. He rocked her slowly until finally, *finally*, she looked up at him. The heat in those light brown eyes told him that he was not alone in this private torture.

There's my angel.

He placed a hand on the small of her back and guided her off the dance floor. They made their way to the bar. The bartender motioned to him. "One more round, Mr. Cardenas? You too, miss?"

Once Sandro gave him the okay, they got settled at a quiet corner of the bar.

"How did you learn to sing like that?" she asked.

"My grandfather listened to old school boleros on the radio while he painted and smoked and smoked and painted. It's basically all he did."

"You have a beautiful voice. Have you considered—"

"No, I'll keep my day job. Thanks. But I'm available for private functions."

She laughed, doing away with all the acrimony of the previous twenty-four hours. Or so he ardently hoped. "Can we start over, Angel?"

Their drinks were served promptly. She reached for hers with a shaky hand. She had not been this nervous back when it was just the two of them at his place.

"Am I asking too much?" he said.

She took a sip from of her cocktail and lowered the glass. "No, you're not. I'd like that, too."

To seal the deal, he leaned close and kissed her.

When the music died down, the band announced a break for the art auction. She pulled her phone out of her purse. "I have to take photos. That's part of my official duties for tonight."

A roster of wealthy people had donated artwork from their private collections. The donors were invited on stage to drum up interest in their offerings. Sandro did not budge. You could not pay him to leave Angel's side. Good thing he didn't have to.

She kept her camera trained to the stage and nudged his flank with an elbow. "Shouldn't you head up there?"

"I sang for them. That should be enough."

"But I want a photo of you."

He reached for her phone, reversed the camera to selfie mode, moved close enough to drop his chin on her shoulder, and snapped a photo of the two of them. "There you go."

She stared at the phone screen a long time. There was no denying they made a handsome couple, Sandro thought. The proof was in her hand.

"I meant for the gallery," she said, her voice thin. "They would love a photo of you with the art."

"They're not going to get it."

"The first piece is a series of photographs titled, *Devastation*," the auctioneer announced. "Here to present it is the artist."

The photographer was a young woman from the Bahamas. She wore a simple white dress and her hair fell in long box braids down her back. After thanking Sandro for the opportunity to address the influential crowd, she spoke of the importance of recording the devastation caused by climate change. "We cannot afford to bury our heads in the sand. Future generations will judge us for our inaction."

Bidding began at fifty thousand dollars. A fierce war between three buyers hiked up the price. The collection of photographs sold for one hundred and ten thousand dollars. Angel recorded it all on video, then switched off her phone and rushed to hug him. The hug was cruelly brief.

"Did you arrange for her to be here tonight?" she said.

"I might've put in a call."

"That's so good of you!" she cried. "This sort of exposure can really help an artist in the long run."

Sandro's mood fell. Everyone was in agreement. He could use his celebrity to lift a struggling artist—or reshape the legacy of a dead one.

She rested a hand on his arm. "Are you okay? Did I say something?"

"*No, querida*. It's fine."

And just as quickly, she withdrew her hand.

Angel flinched as if she'd been burned. He'd called her *querida*. She knew it meant nothing, maybe just another word that he tossed around. But her reaction was over-the-top. She had slept with this man, and yet the unexpected use of an endearment had shot straight to her head.

After the auction, Gigi, Rose and Jenny swarmed them. "Hey, you two! There you are!"

Alessandro let his friends plant kisses on his cheeks and even sample his drink.

"It's a wrap," Gigi said. "We're heading out to meet Jordan at The Zoo. Are you two coming?"

"I can't," Angel said. "I have to work in the morning."

Gigi turned to Alessandro who gave her a pointed look.

She smiled. "I didn't think so. Don't forget tomorrow's party at Garage."

"The club?" Alessandro asked.

"No," Jenny replied. "An actual parking garage. What will these crazy kids come up with next?"

"It's not an ordinary garage," Rose said. "It was designed by Swiss architects."

"Sounds like fun," Alessandro said dryly.

"I'm attending that one," Angel said. "You know, for the gallery."

Alessandro flashed that grin. "In that case it really does sound like fun and I'll be there."

The squad made a grand exit with loud goodbyes and air kisses.

Alessandro turned to her. "Do you need a ride home?"

"I can manage," Angel said. What she meant was: *Take me home. Now!*

"No way I'm putting you in an Uber, if you could even find one."

"Well, there's no rush. I don't have to leave right now." She was acting like an octogenarian, and that wasn't even fair to the eighty-plus crowd. Some might be out partying right now.

The band resumed. Alessandro suggested they find a quiet corner. They wandered off to a remote seating area tucked beyond the cluster of papier-mâché trees.

"I have to ask," he said. "Was I any help?"

"What do you mean?"

"With your rebound efforts. Did I help any?"

Angel nearly spit out her second lychee martini.

"The way you left, I wasn't sure how effective I'd been."

"You know why I left. Let's not go there again."

"You didn't even say thank you," he said, indignant.

"As in…thank you for your service?"

"You wouldn't have to stand on ceremony or anything."

"I wouldn't dream of it."

"I've been dreaming of you."

Angel went soft everywhere. Did he know the effect he had on her? His next careless words proved that he didn't.

"If rebound sex doesn't work out, there's always revenge."

"You've been giving this some thought."

"Have you considered posting that photo of us?"

That quick selfie had astonished her. She and Alessandro looked good together. And not only that, they looked comfortable with each other. A stranger could tell that they were intimate. The fact he'd suggested that she use it as fodder to get back at her stupid ex saddened her. It revealed something about him. He'd grown accustomed to people using his celebrity to further their own causes in both positive and negative ways.

"Thanks for the offer," she said. "You should know that I'd never use you like that."

"What if I want you to?"

Angel set her drink down on a low table and reached for him by the loop of his belt. "Stop."

She did not want to hear any more talk of rebound tactics or revenge plots.

He took her face in his hands; his eyes were as black as the ocean. "Fine. I'll stop, but the offer stands."

"What do you get out of this?" she asked. "Just curious."

"I get you."

"You already have me."

Alessandro crushed her mouth with a kiss. They toppled onto a nearby chaise in a tangle of limbs. He nudged aside the silky ruched bodice of her dress and the lace of her bra. His teeth closed tightly on a nipple. Angel wanted to cry out with pleasure, and then she remembered where they were.

"We can't do this here!"

Alessandro slowly drew away from her. "But we're doing this?"

Now she cupped his face. "If the offer still stands."

He got up and pulled her to her feet. "Let's get out of here."

It was YOLO all the way home, in a convertible with the top down.

Sandro was driving his own car tonight, a compact Alfa Romeo that suited him far better than the borrowed Bentley. The leather seat cradled Angel and the breeze teased her hair. Sandro took on the curves of the highway, one hand on the wheel and the other on the clutch...or on her knees, or burrowed between them, or traveling up the length of her thigh. Angel couldn't wait to get home but she never wanted this ride to end.

By the time they'd made it to her place, Angel was drunk with desire. She had thought the last time was *the* last time. It had been a surreal experience. He was practically a stranger and his touch felt new. How would it be different this time? The man kissing her neck while she fumbled with her keys at her apartment door did not feel like a stranger.

"Need help?"

He meant with her keys, not her mental state.

"Thanks. I can manage."

She could *not* manage. He waited patiently for one second for her to get it together. Then he took the key from her, inserted it into the tricky old lock, and deftly turned it until it clicked. Damn it! Why was that hot?

She ushered him into her living room. "Next you're

going to tell me that you worked as a locksmith before hitting it big."

"A janitor."

"The tenants must have loved you."

She switched on a lamp and lit the candle on the dining table for ambiance. Basically, she did not know what to do. Alessandro roamed around, exploring her space in very much the same fashion that she had explored his. If he were looking for signs of her personality, the only ones he'd find were her potted plants and her framed paintings. Although she liked the furniture, every piece a flea market or Craigslist find, it all belonged to Chris. He had no need for it in Australia.

Angel stepped out of her heels and tossed them onto the rug beneath the midcentury coffee table. When he approached one of her paintings, a simple but colorful landscape hanging over her desk, she went for a quick and easy diversion. Her blue dress joined her sandals on the floor. Alessandro must have heard the whisper of silk because he immediately turned to face her.

"Um… Do you want a house tour, a glass of wine or… what?"

There was something uniquely empowering about being on her home turf.

Alessandro turned his back on the painting. "Option 3, if that's alright."

"Option 3 it is, but you're overdressed."

"I'll take care of it."

While he stripped off his clothes, Angel thought it might be best to shut her blinds. She walked over to the window. He grabbed her by the waist, backed her onto the windowsill and stripped her of her lingerie. Alessandro Cardenas was deliciously naked between her thighs. The man was cut from bronze, all hard planes and sharp angles, and every square inch of him taught and tight. To keep him there, she wrapped her legs around his thighs.

He cupped her face and ran the rough pad of his thumb over her lips. "My angel is bad tonight."

Now, she could admonish him for the simplistic characterization of her sexuality—or she could just be bad.

Angel tightened her legs around him. Fingers woven in her hair, he tugged her head back and kissed her. His hands left her hair and roamed over her body. These were not the hands of a stranger. He knew where and how to touch her, cupping her breasts and teasing her nipples until her back arched and her head slammed against the windowpane.

He slid two fingers inside her. "Did you think about me last night?"

"What?"

"Last night. Did you think about me?"

He was stroking her and her mind was singularly focused on his hands, not his words. "Last night was...last night."

"Now tell me. Why did you run away?"

The truth spiraled out of her. "I was scared."

He rubbed his nose to hers. "Scared of me?"

"Scared of *this*!"

He could do with that information what he liked. She was scared of the pull he had on her. It was pure burning emotion, defying logic or reason, and it made her do the unthinkable.

But Alessandro didn't seem bothered by this revelation. Or maybe he already knew. He seemed to have her figured out. He kissed her again and again while his fingers explored deeper. Angel arched forward knocking a decorative crystal off the edge of the sill. It dropped on his foot. That didn't bother him, either. He laughed it off and pulled her to her feet. "Why can't I ever get you in bed?"

That first night at the penthouse, they'd gotten only as far as the rug on the bedroom floor and crawled into bed afterward where they promptly fell asleep. At least here, at her place, there wasn't too far to travel to find the nearest bed.

Angel led him to her bedroom. Along the way, he stopped to pluck a foil packet from the pocket of his trousers, which he left strung over an armchair. Good thing he'd planned ahead because she didn't have condoms in the apartment. She hadn't needed any for a long, long time.

Her bedroom was dark except for the pale glow of the table lamp in the front room. She poured herself onto her bed, while Alessandro remained standing at the foot. He tore open the foil packet and spoke deliberately. "Yesterday morning, I woke up wanting you. Last night I stayed up fighting the urge to show up at your door. And tonight when I saw you, I knew there was no other possible outcome than this." He looked her square in the eyes. "So, yeah. It's scary, Angeline."

"Don't call me that."

Angel closed her eyes as soon as the words leaped out. What had possessed her?

Alessandro went silent a moment. "Don't use your name?"

"Never mind." She sat up straight and took the condom packet from his hand and finished the job—the less talking the better. "I'm so ready for you."

He eased her onto her back and crawled over her. Angel was murmuring nonsensically. "Yes. Yes. Don't. Yes." He entered her inch by inch, deliberately, cruelly slow.

"What do you want me to call you?"

Her words turned into whimpers.

"If not Angeline, then what?"

Angel gripped his arms. "Forget it."

His tactics were more advanced than hers. With a slight shift in position, he sank in deeper inside her, leaving no room for self-possession. "You like it when I call you Angel? Is that it?"

"Call me yours."

He went still. Angel squeezed her eyes shut again. She was not going to make it through the night.

"My angel..." He brushed his parted lips to hers. "And what does my angel want?"

Angel was near delirious with pleasure. "She wants you."

They'd made love before, but it was in her simple room, her plain bed, that they truly became lovers.

Eleven

"This is the part of the rom-com when you make me pancakes."

"Even if we had the time, I couldn't bring that fantasy to life. I'm no cook. Why do you think I value Myles so much?"

"Protein smoothie it is," she said with a shrug and gave her state of the art blender a whirl.

With the first rays of dawn streaming through Angel's kitchen window, their day began with coffee, quiet conversation and now protein shakes. She was dressed for work, looking elegant in an emerald green dress. Her hair was brushed into a high ponytail and gold hoops hung at her ears. The color in her cheeks and that coy smile were all his doing, or so he liked to think.

Sandro had yet to put on his pants. After their shower, he was feeling lazy. All he wanted was to fold back into bed with her, but she was focused on heading out the door.

Paloma was expecting her at the convention center in an hour. Sandro had offered to drive her to work. She'd accepted with one caveat: he had to drop her off one half block away from the convention center. "I can't be seen with you."

When Sandro thought of the lengths people went to in order to be seen with him, this just cracked him up. "You want to hide this?"

Wearing only his boxer briefs, he turned to give her a look at the goods. Her gaze swept over him appreciatively. Those luminous brown eyes got him every time.

"You're my client," she said.

"I'm more than that."

"No one needs to know that." She poured him a glass of the shake she'd taken such pride in whipping up. "More importantly, Paloma doesn't need to know that. Now drink up and get dressed."

"My poor Angel, how can you stand Paloma?"

"I can't!" she confessed with a horrified laugh. "Which is why I need a new job."

He was relieved to hear it. Gallery Six was shady. He couldn't come out and tell her. For one thing, he had no proof. And what if she let it slip? He did not want to tip off *la Paloma*. "We'll get on that as soon as this fair is done."

"*We* won't be doing anything. You'll be gone and I'll be packing up for Orlando."

He couldn't believe how deeply those words cut him. She was dismissing him and had very concrete plans on how to move on. "This is the first I'm hearing about Orlando."

"That's where I'm from."

"Don't you like it here?"

"I do."

"This apartment is great." He meant it, even though

he was desperately grasping at reasons for her to abort her plans. "I've lived in Miami my whole life, for the most part, and I've never met anyone who actually lived in this area."

"Chris picked this apartment."

Chris...

She took a long sip from her glass as if stalling for time. "It's close to the university's school of marine science," she said, finally.

Ah. Now for whatever reason he didn't think the apartment was so great. It was old and dated. He reached for her hand. "Just so you know, I'm not leaving right away. I'm sticking around awhile."

"Why?"

"Film production delays. Plus, my agent seems to think I need a break."

"Do you need a break?"

They stood at opposite sides of the kitchen island, hands linked. "It wouldn't hurt."

She drained her glass, avoiding his eyes. "I don't leave for Orlando right away. The lease doesn't lapse until March of next year."

He could work with that.

If Sandro were brave enough to be honest, and bold enough to hope, he'd admit that his meeting Angel felt fortuitous. It felt like the beginning of something good—if they didn't mess it up.

Angel took their glasses to the sink. "You know that thing I said last night? I don't know why I had you call me that...it was crazy sex talk."

A lot of crazy sex talk had gone down last night. He wasn't ready to take any of it back.

He grabbed one end of the dishrag she was holding

and used it to draw her to him. "You mean when I called you mine?"

She nodded slowly before putting it in words. "Yes."

Sandro watched her struggle, but he would not relent. "Do you want me to stop?"

"No."

"Come here, my angel."

She melted into his arms. He held and rocked her, stroking her back, until someone simultaneously knocked at her door and rang her doorbell. Then a strident female voice called out, "Angeline!" and a few words in French that he did not understand.

"Angeline! *C'est ta marraine!*"

Damn it all to hell! It was Angel's godmother. Not the "fairy" kind who made your dreams real with a wave of a wand, but the Haitian kind who snooped, meddled and reported back to your mother.

Angel gripped Alessandro's shoulders, her fingers digging into his flesh.

"Listen to me. I want you to go into the bedroom and not make a sound until I come get you. Do you understand?"

The actor gave her a look of hurt betrayal. "You're determined to keep me in the closet."

"We're not yet at the point where you meet my crazy family."

"When do you think we'll get to that point?"

"Never!" Angel said. "Now go and hide. I'll pump up your deflated ego after."

His eyebrows shot up. "By any means necessary?"

She was shaking with bottled-up laughter. He was impossible. "Just go!"

Alessandro blew her a kiss before disappearing into the bedroom. Angel was still grinning when she opened the door to her mother's cousin Hélène Roger, or *Tati* Hélène, as she liked to be called. A petite woman with smooth dark brown skin, she wore pastel pink scrubs and a matching cardigan with a brown leather Coach bag tucked under her arm.

"Tati Hélène! What brings you here so early?"

Her godmother presented her with a pair of stacked Tupperware. "You missed Charles's retirement dinner. I brought you some food."

How thoughtful. But Angel suspected her mother had dispatched her ally to check in on her child who'd been "abandoned" in Miami by the boyfriend that she had never liked in the first place. Stunts like this made her plan to move back home less and less enticing.

"So heavy. What's in this?"

"Just a little something. *Lambi en sauce, salade Russe, macaroni au gratin…*"

"Wow! Thanks!" Conch in Creole sauce, rice and beans, beet and potato salad, and her godmother's famous mac and cheese: a feast in takeout containers. "Sorry to have kept you waiting. I was getting ready for work."

"Is that what you're wearing to work? *Ah, non!*"

Angel glanced down at her dress, purchased on a whim off Instagram. She was headed to the cocktail party in the Swiss-designed parking garage straight after work. The dress struck the right balance with its capped sleeves, bias-cut skirt, and high slit over her right thigh.

"Don't worry," Angel said. "This is very appropriate for an art show."

Before her godmother could tell her to find a "good" job in hospital administration, Angel took the food into the kitchen and arranged the containers in her mostly empty refrigerator. She had no doubt her godmother would be back within a week to collect the prized containers.

"I'll get these back to you," Angel called out from the kitchen. "I promise!"

She returned to the front room to find her aunt examining a pair of tailored black trousers. Angel stopped midstride and came close to toppling forward. She raced through hundreds of possible explanations, settling for the most probable one. "Those belong to Chris."

Tati Hélène shot her a look that said she wasn't born yesterday. "This is quality. Chris never wore anything this nice." She held up the pants as evidence and Angel prayed another condom wouldn't come tumbling out. "That boy only wore khaki pants, even to your cousin's baby shower, and he was *not* this tall."

"That's why he left them behind," Angel said, no longer able to hide her irritation. She was a grown-ass woman in her own rental apartment. Why should she have to explain herself? This would be the part of the sitcom where the main character would tell her busybody godmother to mind her own business. Angel, however, was not born into a sitcom prototype family. Her parents, aunts, uncles, and honorary aunts and uncles were from Haiti. She and her cousins were first generation American who gave their parents ulcers with their "American" lifestyles. Dating, pursuing careers outside of the medical profession, marrying foreigners, and best of all, "living in sin," were all signs that they'd lost their way.

"Tati Hélène," Angel said as respectfully as possible. "I hate to rush you, but I am going to be late for work. You don't want me to *lose* my job."

Those proved to be the magic words. Losing a job, or

pèdi travay, was a calamity no Haitian immigrant would wish upon anyone.

"Okay, okay, I'm leaving." Tati Hélène shuffled to the door. "*Bonne journée, ma cocotte.* And wear a sweater, at least. It's December."

"I will. Don't worry," Angel said. "*Merci* for the dinner. I'll eat it tonight."

With that, Angel ushered her godmother out the door and went to join Alessandro in the bedroom. He was standing by her dresser studying a painting on the wall. It was one of her few from childhood, a bougainvillea vine creeping over a cement wall. Angel handed him his pants. She wondered how much he'd heard or understood of her conversation with her godmother, but the devilish grin he flashed her confirmed that he'd heard and understood *everything*.

He fell onto the bed and joined his hands behind his head. "There better be enough food for two."

Angel rolled onto the bed and cuddled next to him. "That was just a preview of my family. Trust me, you wouldn't want to meet them."

He tucked her to him. When he answered his tone was surprisingly solemn. "I would, actually. Family is important."

She raised herself onto her elbow and studied the near-naked man in her bed, seeing him with newfound appreciation. Chris had never wanted to spend time with her rambunctious family. Toward the end of their relationship, she'd had to resort to bribery. "Come with me to my cousin's baby shower and I'll go with you to see the hundredth *Star Wars* movie."

He smoothed her hair. "Come on, let's go. I don't want you to lose your job."

Angel checked her watch. "I'm going to be late, and Paloma will kill me."

"No way. I'll get you there on time."

And he did.

Twelve

"We cannot certify the authenticity of *El Jardín Secreto*." The expert had called while Sandro was running lines over Zoom with his acting coach.

He stepped out onto the terrace for privacy, even though he was home alone. The authenticator explained in detail how they'd come to their conclusion.

"It all comes down to red paint?"

"That particular pigment was not commercially available until 1985. There's no way your grandfather could have found it for such liberal use ten years earlier."

The blooming bougainvillea flowers had betrayed the secrets of the garden. Funny.

"We wish we had better news for you, Mr. Cardenas."

"It's the news I expected."

Over the last few days, Sandro had managed to put the painting out of his mind. He hadn't wanted the results back this soon, either. It forced him to link Angel to the gallery that sold him a forged copy of his own grandfather's painting, a thing he did not want to do.

"Most professionals would try to avoid this common mistake. This leads me to think we're not dealing with a professional. How would you like to proceed?"

"I'm not sure."

"You may file a police report. We find that most of our clients don't."

Most wouldn't for the reasons Paloma had so eloquently explained. They wouldn't want their neighbors to know they'd been conned.

"More often than not these cases are not prosecuted, even with the best of evidence," the authenticator continued. "Either way, our discretion is guaranteed."

Sandro ended the call and pocketed his phone. The cloudy morning sky mirrored his mood. Who would go through the trouble of reproducing the old man's paintings? Who had suddenly expressed interest in their market value? And called him out for not doing more to increase it? All signs pointed to his brother. Sandro wasn't delusional. Ed didn't have the skill to reproduce an original stick figure, let alone an oil painting. But he could have hired someone to reproduce the paintings and pass them off to galleries. You didn't have to be a genius to work out that plan.

He was going to have to pay his big brother a visit.

Two hours later, Sandro landed in Tampa. Good thing his brother's tire shop wasn't too far from the airport. A driver was waiting to take him there and back. The car hadn't slowed to a stop when he pushed open the door. When he burst into the small shop, welcomed by the smell of grease and rubber, his brother proved that Sandro wasn't the only one with theatrical inclinations.

"Well if it isn't the King of Hollywood!" Eddy bellowed from behind the cash register. "To what do we owe this honor?"

The few customers threw glances their way, but none likely recognized him. He was just another Latino guy in the ball cap, sunglasses and bland T-shirt. "We need to talk."

"Nah," Eddy replied. "I need to take care of my customers."

"Eddy," Sandro said through clenched teeth. "I came a long way."

"Is that right?" Eddy said. "Well, take a damn number."

Balding, paunchy, with a lined face, Eddy looked older than the seven years he had on Sandro. But he'd had a difficult life. Their father's death had hit him harder. Sandro was only four at the time and had been living with JD since he was two. In the family, they said their dad had died of stubbornness, having refused to go to the ER when a minor cut turned into a raging infection. Sandro was deemed too young to attend the funeral. All he knew was that his father, like his mother, had stopped coming around. It was complicated, as was his relationship with this half brother whom he had once worshipped.

Sandro went over to the waiting area and flipped open a frayed copy of *Car and Driver*. He was going to sit here until—

The staged sit-in didn't last long. Eddy waved him over. His office was down the hall. It was large enough for a desk and not much else. Still, Eddy had managed to squeeze in a recliner for himself.

"Welcome to my humble abode. Have a seat."

Sandro lowered himself onto one of the two guest seats that lined the wall. There was little legroom, but he made it work.

"Coffee? Tea? Or what do you guys drink in California? Green lettuce juice? Is that it?"

"I'm good, thanks."

"Yeah. I can tell you're good."

"Why the attitude?" Sandro asked, point blank.

"It's not about nothing," Eddy said. "You show up here unannounced. You don't ask about Linda."

"Oh? How is she, by the way?"

"She's a certified substitute teacher."

"Give her my best."

"I will."

"Can we knock this off now?"

Their relationship had not been considered loving. As the illegitimate child of their dad and his mistress, Sandro was by default the black sheep. The power dynamic had shifted over recent years, with Sandro gaining confidence and asserting himself.

"Sabina tells me you two have talked about JD's paintings, wanting to see them in the world."

"Don't know why you're hiding them. Are you embarrassed?"

"Don't go there," Sandro said quietly.

Eddy looked down at the points of his shoes. "Just asking."

"What do you care? You've never cared."

"That's what I don't like. Righteous attitude. You're not the only one who loved JD."

"I don't question that. Just your interest in the paintings."

"I've got no interest in the damn paintings. You've seen to that."

"Seeing how you've wiped out more than half of them, I don't know how you can complain."

"There you go, blaming me for that fire again!"

"Whose cigarette was it?"

"It was an accident."

"You tossed a cigarette into a shed full of turpentine and other explosives."

"It was an accident," Eddy repeated.

Straight after their grandfather's wake, his friends had gathered in the yard outside JD's painting shed. One tossed cigarette had set the shed ablaze. "Accident or not, the result is the same."

"Why are you here?" Eddy asked. "You didn't come all this way to fight about the fire or JD's paintings."

"Actually, yeah, I did."

Sandro opened the duffel bag he'd brought with him and pulled out *El Jardín Secreto*. He dropped the painting on Eddy's cluttered desk.

"What's this?"

"A fake."

"No me jodas," Eddy murmured. "How do you know?"

"An expert analyzed it."

"How does the expert know?"

"That's what he does."

"Or he's taking your money and feeding you bull."

"It's a fake."

"Okay…so what?" Eddy said. "What do you expect me to do about it?" Sandro stared at him. "You think I have something to do with it? You think I have an art studio at the back of the shop?"

"I'm not saying that. Just wondering if you know anything about it."

"I don't."

"Are you sure?"

"Get outta here with this mess! You show up—unannounced—and freaking ruin my day."

"Sorry," Sandro said, unfazed. "That wasn't my intention."

"The result is the same."

Sandro did not budge. He sat stewing in frustration. This was plainly going nowhere, but was he really going to leave without answers?

Eddy shooed him off like a stray dog. "Go on! I got a shop to run!"

The shop was nearly empty. There was no way Sandro could remind him of that without coming off as an ass. He stood to go.

"And take that with you," Eddy said, sliding the painting across the desk with the tip of a logo pen. "Don't plant it on me."

Just when Sandro reached for it, Eddy stopped him. "Wait." He studied the painting for a long moment, his eyes wistful.

"What is it?" Sandro asked.

Eddy shook his head. "Like I said—you weren't the only one who loved JD's work."

Sandro snatched the painting off the desk and shoved it back into his bag. "It's a fake. Remember that?"

"Says you and your expert," Eddy said. "But you gotta admit. If it's a fake, it's a damn good one."

"I'll pass that message along when we catch the forger."

"You won't."

"Why do you say that?"

"A hunch."

Sandro leaned against the doorway. "A hunch?"

"Who really cares, anyway?"

"Someone is making money off JD. That doesn't piss you off?"

"Imitation is the sincerest form of whatever."

"Bullshit!"

"Here's some advice."

"I'm listening."

"Go back to California or Cannes or wherever you spend your time. We've got enough problems. Leave us nobodies alone."

The question was cued up, ready to roll off his tongue. *Do you hate me that much?* Only he knew Eddy didn't hate him. He envied him, and that was just as bad. This shop had been his older brother's dream and he'd built it from ground up with little help from anyone. Sandro couldn't imagine him living any other life yet the resentment was there, palpable, weaving itself within their conversations. Eddy had been fine with him being a struggling actor, waiting tables and cleaning rest rooms. Sandro was often the butt of jokes at holiday reunions. So much so that he had stopped attending. Once his career picked up, though, Eddy's attitude changed. The entrepreneur now referred to himself as a "nobody." Ridiculous.

Sandro turned to leave. "Good seeing you again."

"You look good, bro!" Eddy called out. "Keep up with that keto diet!"

Thirteen

"That seems to me like an unfair cultural appropriation…"

A string bean of a man in a tweed jacket frowned at a painting of an American pop star reimagined as Ganesha. Angel bit back a smile and wandered to the next exhibit. On her half-hour break she liked to wander through the halls, soaking up as much art as possible. The next room featured a life-size glass house. The manager was on his mobile phone, hustling. "We're everywhere. So wherever you want to be, we can get you there."

Angel felt a tug at her heart. Was that how it felt to be celebrated, promoted and valued? That sort of overture could potentially take an artist from anonymity to hot commodity. That was the dream that she had walked away from. She had locked away those ambitions to embrace her new career path. So much so, she hadn't even wanted Alessandro to look at her paintings. She hoped to keep her failures hidden, if only for the short while they had together. Things didn't have to get that deep.

Her phone buzzed in her hand. Alessandro had sent her a photo, and all the overconceptualized artwork in the convention center faded to black. It was a screenshot of an Instagram post from two summers back. He was standing on a dock at Fisher Island wearing a black T-shirt and cargo shorts.

She'd saved his phone number under the name BEST MALE LEAD. The text message that followed read: I look good in shorts, too.

Angel was fully aware that she was texting and flirting like her teenaged self. That awareness didn't prevent her from throwing herself into it.

ANGEL'S PHONE: I like you best without pants.

BEST MALE LEAD: My wicked Angel... I'll be late for the parking garage party.

ANGEL'S PHONE: Long day in paradise?

BEST MALE LEAD: Difficult day. Won't bore you with details.

Angel stared at her phone. She wished he would bore her with details. She wanted to know the not-so-glamorous side of him. What wore him down? What weighed on his mind?

BEST MALE LEAD: Please don't run off with another guy.

ANGEL'S PHONE: This is a work event. I'm not going to cruise celebrities.

BEST MALE LEAD: Celebrities don't worry me. It's those starving artists...

ANGEL'S PHONE: Ah! The ones with goatees...

BEST MALE LEAD: I used to be a starving artist.

ANGEL'S PHONE: No goatee?

BEST MALE LEAD: Didn't need one. It would be a crime to hide this face. May I take you home later tonight?

ANGEL'S PHONE: I'll think about it.

BEST MALE LEAD: Think about me without pants.

Angel laughed. The real crime would be to not take this man home tonight.

1010 Alton Road resembled a cement origami structure. It cost the owner fifty million dollars to build and the average motorist thirty dollars to park. The ground floor was dedicated to retail space. But the party was held on the top floor. It was redesigned as a sculpture garden against the backdrop of unobstructed views of Miami Beach. In short, it was fabulous.

A popular DJ was spinning, so there would be no surprise live performances tonight. She was grateful; her heart couldn't take it. But she was excited beyond reason to see Alessandro again. No matter that they'd been apart for only a few hours. She was even excited to see his crew of friends. Angel stood at the entrance and scanned the crowd composed of collectors, curators and the artists that they all coveted. A few people outside the industry caught

her eye: a street-style photographer and his fashion blogger girlfriend, a famed performance artist and activist,
and an art critic for the *Times*.

And there he was.

Another thing her heart couldn't take? Seeing her "date"
and his ex huddled up in a corner. Although the woman
had her back to him, Angel recognized her right away from
her famous cropped blue hair. Actress/musician Chloe
London was one of Alessandro's most famous exes.

In a stunning plot twist, after all the drama about Chris,
he was the one to introduce an evil ex. Although there was
no evidence that Chloe London was evil, apart from the
fact that she'd starred as an evil witch in a Disney movie.
But by all accounts, except maybe that of Alessandro's
publicist, the breakup had been brutal.

Angel did not know what to do with herself. Thankfully, a waiter swung by and offered her a glass of champagne, which gave her something to do with her hands.
She was being ridiculous, overly dramatic and a touch pos-
sessive. In his world, where there were no rules, he could
do what he wanted. There would always be something or
someone more exciting to catch his attention.

Angel could map her thoughts from the dangerous turn
they had taken to the ditch where they were headed. Pump
the brakes! She was here for work—even if her work consisted of snapping a few photos for the gallery's Instagram account.

And then Alessandro looked up. While nodding in
agreement at whatever Chloe was saying, he scanned the
entrance as if searching for someone. When his gaze settled
on her, he brightened and the search appeared to be over.

Sandro hadn't thought he'd make it back from Tampa on
time, but good thing he had. He would not have wanted to

miss Angel's grand entrance. She stopped his heart in her "nothing" dress paired with tall suede boots. He stirred with impatience, eager to get away from Chloe and to get his hands on Angel. He listened as Chloe updated him on the recent shenanigans of her toy poodle. Then he begged off as tactfully as possible. He'd lost sight of Angel for a moment and when he finally spotted her, her quiet anxiety roared loud in his ears.

What was she thinking?

"Hey, you," he greeted.

He refrained from touching her. She'd made it clear that they weren't "out." And he was okay with it. Really, he was. Once the press got wind of their affair, things would get complicated very quickly. Flying under the radar was likely the smartest thing to do. He only wished that she weren't so adamant about it.

She gave him an empty smile. "Hey! You made it."

"I couldn't wait to see you." Sandro hadn't even gone back to the island to change. He'd thrown a blazer over his T-shirt and jeans and hoped his smile made up for it. "If your godmother saw you without a sweater, I'm not sure she'd approve."

That got her laughing. And he was relieved, mainly because he had a clue as to what might have triggered her initial reaction.

"You're not going to let this die down, will you?"

"I love your godmother."

"You love that she loved your pants."

"That, too." He motioned for her to follow him. "Come with me. I found a private spot for us to talk behind that giant penis."

Angel whimpered with suppressed laughter, her eyes bright with tears. "You're the big penis! It's a statue of a double helix!"

"It's whatever you say it is. You're the expert."

He drew her close and hugged her, rubbing the small of her back. "Have you eaten, babe?"

"I'm sure there's a bacon-wrapped date with my name on it somewhere."

There was more than that. He'd checked out the spread. "I'll make sure you're fed," he promised. "Everything okay, otherwise."

"Everything is fine." She eased away from him. "And you?"

"Yeah," he said with a shrug.

She nodded. "Cool."

He couldn't stand it, all the things they weren't saying were piling up. Sandro cut through it and addressed the "ex" in the room. "That was Chloe London I was speaking with just now. We used to…" He couldn't finish the sentence. What had he and Chloe been up to those few months they were together? Killing time?

"We don't have to go there," she said. "It's fine."

It wasn't fine. "You're big on rules. How about this for one? We tell each other the things that matter." When she moved to protest, he stopped her. "Don't tell me this doesn't matter."

She grabbed his hand. "I'm trying to tell you it's not necessary. The press coverage was thorough."

"The press?" According to the "press," Chloe had cheated and dumped him for her ex. It was no wonder Angel didn't want to talk about it.

"You shouldn't believe everything you read online."

"It wasn't online, it was in *Vanities*."

Sandro stepped back. Her hand slipped from his. He was so offended that he switched to Spanish. *No me digas que crees—*"

She reclaimed his hand. "I told you the sordid details

about my breakup. It's only fair that you get to share yours."

"There was no breakup," he said. "We were never together, not in a real way. I had time on my hands and she was on a break from Tyler. When they got back together, I was filming in Toronto."

Angel's expressive face went blank and he understood his mistake. "It's nothing like us."

"Isn't it?" she said. "Some brokenhearted woman needs a distraction and you offer yourself up as a chew toy." She poked him in the ribs to drive the point home. "You're not a chew toy for the brokenhearted."

"Is that what you are?" Sandro asked. "Brokenhearted?"

With Chloe the answer to this question didn't bother him. She was a good person with a kind heart, but her thing with Tyler was their business. He hadn't cared enough to get entangled in it. But with Angel, it weighed on him a little too heavily. He hated that she was still stuck on her ex. She only had to mention him and jealousy shred his insides. Plus he could not remember the last time he'd had to compete for a woman's attention and he was clumsy at it. His flippant offers for rebound sex were nothing but a facade, a lid covering a pool of want. He wanted her. Why couldn't he just say, "I like you"?

Sandro leaned against the penis statue, wondering when and where exactly he'd lost his balls. He missed it when Angel's cool nonchalance turned to hot anger.

"I was never brokenhearted, you big dummy!"

He snapped to attention. "Okay..."

"Chris and I were on our last legs by the time he left. We weren't talking. We weren't having fun. We weren't much involved in each other's lives. If I'd had my act together, I would've left him long ago."

He stopped her. "Angel, the look on your face when you got that alert."

There was nothing an ex could post that could upset him if his feelings weren't involved. He certainly wouldn't sign up for alerts.

"I was upset, yes!" she admitted openly. "It was an intrusion. I was just getting to know you and it pulled me into the past. What bothered me, really, was the way he'd ended things. As if he were destined for greatness and I was dead weight dragging him down. It was humiliating. And I felt like…"

She struggled with the last word. Sandro said it, so she wouldn't have to. "A failure."

She nodded. "I'm thirty. That's an age when you ought to have your shit together."

"I wouldn't know about that."

She groaned. "At thirty you worked three jobs."

"And had four roommates."

She made a face. "That sounds terrible."

He kissed her; it was long overdue. "It was terrible."

"Maybe in the spirit of competition, I got obsessed with keeping score. I used Chris as a visual aid. His videos showed me how far off track I was."

"Or you think you were," he corrected.

She made a gesture as if to say, tomato/tomahto, it was all the same.

"Hate to say this, but Chris reminds me of this tool." He knocked on the double helix penis and she burst out laughing. His fear that they'd taken things too far tonight gently subsided. He drew her tight and kissed her as if they were alone, back at his house or her apartment, and not at a raging party with a frenetic DJ upping the ante with every track. He wanted to get out of here, but she still had work to do. He couldn't keep her tucked away for much longer.

Just as he was about to propose they rejoin the party, she held him tighter. "I've never told any of this to anyone."

"Oh, my angel…" He felt honored, flat-out honored, that she had trusted him enough to confide in him. "I'll keep your secrets."

She whispered back. "And I'll keep yours, just so you know. You can tell me anything."

Had they just exchanged vows? Exciting…

"Listen to me." He eased her away and gripped her shoulders. "I've lived in California long enough to know that we have to end this session with an affirmation."

She laughed, all the while wiping at her eyes with the back of her hands. "Alessandro, you're the only one who can make me laugh and cry at the same time."

Good, he thought. It was a sign that he was getting to the heart of her. "Repeat after me. I'm not a failure."

She took a deep breath. "I'm not a failure."

"Good girl."

"Not so fast! Now it's your turn," she said. "Repeat after me. You're no one's chew toy."

Over the years, Sandro had coupled up and split up more times than he could count. His work always came first. He could always count on his friends to fill the time between jobs. His life had been a wild spin and he'd enjoyed it. Angel made him want to step off the carousel.

"I'm no one's chew toy, except yours."

She rolled her eyes at him, but he could tell that she loved it. "That's progress, I guess."

"Some might call it a major breakthrough."

"They'd be wrong," she said. "Now come on. You promised to feed me. Let's go."

She'd grabbed his hand and didn't let go, not even after they'd emerged from their hiding place. They made a meal of the array of appetizers and, an hour later, were still holding hands when Gigi, Rose and Jenny made their grand entrance. Sandro held her purse while she went around snapping the photos for her gallery's social media accounts. Finally, when she was done, she curled an arm around his neck and whispered, "Take me home."

In the elevator, at his request, she raised the hem of her dress to show him how far high those sleek boots reached. He pinched her thigh. She laughed all the way down to the ground floor valet station. But Alessandro kept sinking deeper into an emotion that he was afraid to identify.

ART BASEL BABE WATCH

So far, the men have brought the heat during Basel. Top on our list is Alessandro Cardenas. Although he has not yet been spotted at the after-hour clubs with his usual crew, here he is on opening night looking like a boss in a Tom Ford suit. Next, the actor sports a more casual look, in a black shirt and trousers, while serenading some lucky girl at The High Tide. Is there nothing this man can't do? Obviously not! We hear that there are some production delays with his next feature. Here's hoping that he spends his free time on the beach, so we can catch a glimpse of the body under the clothes. #SandroFever

—*@Sunshine&Wine_IG*

COMMENTS:
@thebitterandthesweet: Who is the basic chick he's serenading?

Fourteen

Art Basel, closing night...

Someone ripped the banana straight off the wall, peeled it and gobbled it down to the great consternation of the crowd. There went the most photographed banana in the world. It was instantly proclaimed performance art.

Paloma sold *YOLO* to a young gay couple from Lisbon.

Justine was feeling well enough to attend the night's big party, albeit with a foot in an orthopedic boot. Which meant Angel had the night off. As soon as she learned the news, she called Alessandro.

He answered on the second ring. "Tell me you were there when that guy ate the banana."

"Ugh! I didn't make it in time." She'd heard the commotion, but Gallery Six's viewing room was halfway across the convention center. "I got a picture of the duct tape on the wall. It's posted on Instagram."

"Good job," he said. "So, what's on the agenda tonight?"

"Nothing! I have the night off."

"Angel…" he said in his teasing way. "Don't play with my emotions."

"I wouldn't!"

She had made it to the break area: an indoor park complete with artificial trees and a spread of fake grass. She took a seat on a bench.

"I'm taking you out," he said. "What would you like to do? Just tell me and I'll make it happen."

Angel turned the question in her mind. "There's one thing."

"What?"

"We'd have to move beyond Basel," she said, dropping her voice to a whisper. "Only the top one percent of artists gets the chance to show here. For the rest, it's every man for himself."

"Or woman," he said.

"No," she said. "It's even worse for women. Say nothing of the nonbinary! Nobody cares!"

"I care," he said. "And I can't go to another Basel party, I swear to God. I'm done. Let's branch out. Want to go to Wynwood?"

She was always taken aback at how well he knew the city. She had half expected him to suggest Ocean Drive. "And Little Haiti. There's an art scene there, too."

"Just you, me and my driver," he said. "Is that alright?"

"I don't know," she said. "Are you sure you want to be out with someone as basic as me?"

She heard him snap to attention, or had he dropped the phone? "Why would you say that?"

"It was a joke," she said. "Someone left a comment on an Instagram post and—"

"*No me digas*, Angel!" he said. "What are you doing reading comments?"

Increasingly, he broke out in Spanish. Angel wondered if this meant that he was more comfortable around her. She hoped that was the case, even though now he was clearly exasperated.

"It was right there. There was no missing it."

"I pay someone to monitor social media," he said. "It doesn't look like I'm missing out on much. Who would call you basic? You're so beautiful, half the time I can't even look at you."

Angel hadn't been fishing for a compliment, but Lord, she'd caught Moby Dick. "It didn't bother me, really. My self-esteem is rock solid."

"Alright," he said, although he didn't sound convinced. "So…you, me and my driver. Sounds good?"

She rose from the bench. Her break was nearly over and Paloma would kill her if she returned late again. "Sounds great."

"Angel, have you met Gus?"

"We've met," Angel said. "You were waiting at the dock when I arrived that first night."

Gus was bearded, bald and built like a linebacker. Angel understood that "driver" was code for "bodyguard." For Alessandro to venture into the city on a warm December night, he needed security. Was this something that she would have to get comfortable with? *No, Angel! Stop! Dead end ahead!* Alessandro would be leaving soon enough. She'd register with a dating app and find a nice boyfriend who did not need an armed guard on a date. The end.

Was Gus armed?

Alessandro took her by the waist and guided her into the car. "First stop Wynwood?"

She agreed. "I don't know where you'll park this beauty."

"It's arranged," Gus said. "We have a spot in a garage."

By "garage" Gus had meant an actual mechanic shop owned by a buddy of his and located one block away from the popular Wynwood Walls. The Alfa Romeo pulled up to a metal drop gate smeared with graffiti. It rose to allow them passage and fell like an iron curtain behind them. The garage owners rushed forward to greet Alessandro and escorted their trio through the front of the shop and out onto the sidewalk. Although it was dark, Alessandro slipped on sunglasses. They were like any other couple, strolling hand in hand, with a bodyguard in tow.

Every square inch of Wynwood was coated in spray paint. Every back alley brick wall was a street artist's canvas. The murals varied in style, but the point was to provoke. Whether it was a pair of widespread angel wings or a play on a political slogan, all that mattered was that it stood out. With so much art on the streets, they avoided the galleries, preferring to stroll the sidewalks.

Angel squeezed her date's hand. She was of average height when surrounded by average people, but at his side, she felt small and dainty. Then Alessandro popped the traditional third date question: "Your place or mine?"

"Well…mine, obviously. Yours is an ocean away."

"It's across the bay, not the straits," he said. "I can get you back in time for work in the morning if you're concerned."

That was always a concern. But she had an idea. "I open the gallery in the morning, but I have the next two days off."

He pulled her into a side street—with Gus standing guard. "Two whole days? No obligations?"

"None."

"Then what's to stop you from coming with me to paradise?"

His gaze lingered on her mouth, anticipating her answer. Angel couldn't help licking her lips. "Nothing."

He kissed her full on the mouth. "Pack a bag. But don't pack too much—you won't need it."

They'd made it to the main attraction. "The Walls" was an outdoor grand scale art space for graffiti and street art. Securing a wall was a competitive process and some of the world's most celebrated artists had been featured. Alessandro mentioned that he'd attended the grand opening. "No one thought it would take off like this."

They stood before a mural of a bird perched on barbwire. The bird had blood-red feathers and his eyes were dots of coal. The opposing wall was painted pink with the words *I'm beautiful, damn it!* Mothers and daughters, sisters and girl squads waited in line for a chance to pose for photos, using the mural as a backdrop.

"This is how people consume art now," Angel said. "It's more immediate and interactive. Much better than a stuffy gallery."

Alessandro looked at her, his expression soft. "Do you like your job at Gallery Six?"

Angel laughed nervously. "You asked me that already."

She'd done a competent job for the gallery these last few days. Was he picking up some other vibe?

"Your answer was bull, and you know it. I want the truth."

She scrounged around for some scraps of truth. "Let's just say, it wasn't my first career choice. I'm still new at it.

The gallery itself is a bit much and a little too concerned with its celebrity clientele—no offense."

He took none. In fact, he seemed relieved.

"Look," she said. "I just need something to work. Okay?"

"Okay."

They migrated to the next mural, a dazzling geometric abstract which, upon close inspection, was composed exclusively of stick figures in various sexual positions. Angel could not focus on it. She was stuck on something he'd said. How had he known her first answer was BS? At the time, they hadn't known each other that long.

"How do you know me so well?"

He shoved his hands in the back pockets of his jeans, feigning boyish innocence. "Reading your body language is not the same as knowing you."

"You always get to the heart of me."

He cocked his head, coal black eyes steady on her. "That's the objective."

He was so damn sexy! Angel forgot where she was and, more importantly, whom she was with. She took his face between her hands and drew him into a kiss.

Their audience swooned.

They were not an average couple on an average date. They were tropical fish in an aquarium, floating around to the amazement and astonishment of a crowd. Someone shouted: "That's Sandro!" A woman screeched: "I knew it!… Who's the girl?"

Alessandro groaned. "Blown cover. Let's go."

That proved to be difficult. The crowd pressed around them. Gus tactfully drilled a tunnel for them to move forward. Armed security guards rushed forward to assist. Sandro appeased his fans with handshakes, smiles, and kisses blown into the air. Angel was in shock. Up until now, their public outings had been limited to controlled environments where celebrities like him were free to roam outside of their gilded cages.

The garage was not far. They were able to duck in and disappear.

"This doesn't always happen," Alessandro said apologetically. "Most times I blend into a crowd."

Angel was doubtful. Could this be his one blind spot? Once upon a time, he might have blended into a crowd like this, but not anymore. She wondered who among his friends would volunteer to tell him the truth.

"Where to now?" he asked.

"You're up for more?"

"Baby, the night is young!"

The endearment tossed out casually set off a glitter bomb in her chest. *What has this man done to me?* Angel had to do better. She couldn't let him get to her like this. What was she going to do when their love affair ended with a great big Hollywood kiss?

They all climbed into the car.

"Where to?" Gus asked.

"*Papaya* on Northwest Second Avenue," Angel replied. The gallery showcased Haitian art and she would be remiss not to stop by during Art Basel week.

"I know it," Gus said. "Let's go."

"We call Gus 'GPS' behind his back," Alessandro said.

"And to my face," Gus chimed good-humoredly.

It was the last Angel heard his voice during the ride. The city was marred with traffic and the short drive took longer than it normally would. Nestled close to Alessandro in the back of the car, fingers intertwined and speaking softly, Angel didn't mind.

"Before we were so rudely interrupted, you were going

to tell me all your secrets," he said, speaking in that quiet way of his that made her tremble.

"Funny. That's not how I remember it."

"Here's your chance," he said. "Tell me something real. Not the stuff I can guess at, but what you keep hidden from everyone."

There were no skeletons drying out in Angel's closet, only her twin pet demons: inadequacy and failure.

Gus turned onto 2nd Avenue. Located at the corner, Papaya was as colorful as its name. The exterior walls were painted a rich apricot hue. Hand-painted palm trees soared up its facade from the ground to the roof. The one-story building blended nicely with its surroundings. The mini-mart next door was peacock blue with the words *BON APPÉTIT BONNE SANTÉ* stenciled in gold, a neighboring property's privacy wall featured religious iconography in primary colors, and the restaurant across the street was a vibrant red.

It occurred to Angel that there was something she could share with Alessandro. *Papaya*, her favorite art gallery, was the appropriate place to do it. But now that they'd finally arrived, Angel had second thoughts.

Fifteen

The goal was to get to the heart of her. Yet whenever he tried, asking direct yet simple questions, she looked as if she might crawl out of her skin. Whatever she was hiding behind her painted facade was tormenting her, and he hated it. To force it would be a mistake. So he let questions go unanswered and tried to read the coded messages in those steady brown eyes that still got to him, even now.

So far, he'd gathered that deep inside she felt like a failure. Tonight, he learned that she desperately needed *something* to work. Having been there himself, he knew it was a dark place to be.

They'd arrived at the gallery. "Let's go."

She grabbed his arm just as he prepared to bolt out of the car. "Wait! I should walk you through this."

The neighborhood was hosting an art walk. She stared out the window at the lively party scene. Sandro was slightly offended. Did she think the Little Haiti crowd would scare him? Or did she worry he'd reject the art she took so much pride in? Either way, he had to stomp those fears.

"I grew up in the Little River area just miles from here," he said. "You're not going to explain anything to me."

"Wow." She released him. "Is there no situation you can't spin with a folksy tale of your humble roots?"

"Apparently not."

Angel was actually wringing her hands. "I might have hyped it up a bit," she said. "This is not a fancy gallery by any stretch. But I want to support them."

"Okay, let's support them."

"Whoa!" She gripped his arm again, tighter this time. "By *support* I mean showing appreciation for their work. Please don't think I brought you here to buy out their inventory."

"Angel! You're taking the fun out of this."

"I'm just saying! You tend to show off a little."

He tended to show off a lot. That was the performer in him. But he didn't have to buy out a business's inventory to show his support. "If I like something, I'll buy it. Plus, there are other things I can do."

"Like what?"

"You'll see." He opened the car door, stepped out and assisted Angel. She was dressed simply in a silky blue top, which she wore with fitted jeans and barely there sandals. Her brown waves gathered at the top of her head with a clip. Although she was not one to layer on clothes, he had already formulated a plan how to best undress her when he finally got her alone. The jeans would have to go first. The top would fall away once he tugged at the ties at the nape of her neck. Then he'd snatch away that hair clip. He imagined her waves would cascade around her shoulders.

Only then would he work on the lacy strapless bra that he'd gotten glimpses of earlier.

But first they had to get through this gallery tour. It meant something to her, and he was going to show up for it.

The glossy Alfa Romeo standing idle at the curb had drawn some attention. When Alessandro and Angel emerged from it, excitement crackled through the gathering crowd. He was not as famous as Angel seemed to think. He was nowhere near a household name. Most people struggled to remember his name or recall which movie they'd seen him in. He hoped his next movie, a big budget adaptation from a popular fantasy trilogy, would change that. He could have ducked into the gallery before anyone had figured out who he was, but he gave it a minute. Soon enough, a young woman cried, "I love you, Sandro!"

Without missing a beat, he called out, "Love you, too!"

And that triggered an uproar and a blaze of flashing camera phone lights. Before they got swamped, he grabbed Angel's hand and headed inside. A security guard ushered them into the reception area and locked the door behind them. He turned to Angel and met her knowing gaze.

"I know what you did there."

"I don't know what you mean."

"Tomorrow's headline will be Hollywood Discovers Artsy Gallery in Little Haiti."

He bent forward and kissed the tip of her nose. "Or something like that."

She mouthed the words *thank you*. Sandro wanted to kiss those lush lips. He could hardly wait to get her back on Fisher Island. All that time alone together, he might die of happiness.

When they entered the first viewing room, the gallery owner nearly fell off the stack of wood crates where he sat, drinking beer from a bottle and chatting with friends.

He knew Angel and extended a warm welcome. He gave them the tour and explained the objective of the space was to promote up-and-coming artists, boost the culture and build community. The paintings were not unlike those his grandfather might have painted, scenes of Caribbean life, beaches, gardens, outdoor markets, women in recline, women at work, women dressed in white, dancing to bongo drums. Sandro took a moment to speak with the night's featured artist who was eager to share that he had been to Cuba last year as part of a cultural exchange program. Sandro posed for photos with the artist, the owner, the security guard and nearly everyone else who'd found themselves locked in the small gallery space with them. All the while Angel was beaming at him. He'd do it all again if it made her look at him like that.

When the frenzy died down, she asked the owner if they could have some time alone in one of the smaller viewing rooms. The space was immediately cleared out. As soon as a pocket door slid shut to offer them ultimate privacy, she backed him against a wall and kissed him fiercely. His hands found their way under the hem of her silky top, in search of skin. Was a gallery tour all it took to get her hot?

"You are so easy," he said when she broke away.

"And you were so good out there!"

"I wasn't putting on an act," he admitted. "This art is more accessible than half the things at Basel. It's the sort my grandfather would make."

"It's the sort my parents would hang on their walls." She pointed to a still life of tropical fruit. Bananas, oranges, pineapples, watermelon and mangoes were lumped into a large basket. The colors were subtle, all shades of yellow and green. "As a kid, I used Crayola paints to copy still life portraits like this one. I made copies of the art in my family home. That's how I taught myself to paint. I worked hard to re-create them, almost obsessively. They were more beautiful and interesting than anything in my coloring books."

Copy... Re-create...

A question fell from him. "You paint?"

"I have a masters in fine arts to prove it," she said with a sad little smile. "Not that I'm doing much with it."

"Those paintings in your apartment...?"

She turned away from him, nodding.

"Why didn't you ever say anything?"

"What's to say? The thing I dedicated my life to is nothing more than a hobby now."

"Why did you quit?"

She did not answer. Could this be the secret that she had been hiding so deeply? A hidden shame? He took her gently by the shoulders and made her face him. Tears glazed her eyes.

He pulled her close. "Don't cry, my angel. It's okay."

She spoke into his shirt. "This is stupid! I'm over it. Really, I am."

Sandro couldn't let her lie to herself. "No, you're not, babe."

She gripped at his sleeves. "Why can't you lie to me?"

Sandro held her tight, laughter rumbling through their bodies. He kissed her hair. Later, he'd ask for more details. He might suggest that she had given up too soon. He'd encourage her to try again. For now, though, he'd rock her and make her laugh. He'd quiet the voice repeating her words.

I worked hard to re-create them, almost obsessively...

The emotional heavy lifting had taken its toll. They dropped Gus off at his downtown condo and drove to her apartment in silence. Back at her place, Angel poured him a glass of ice water and straightened things out in the kitchen. Then she headed to her room, promising to slip into something more comfortable if he were good.

"I'll be good!" he assured her.

Sandro circled the living/dining/home office area while he waited. She kept the light to one source, a table lamp near the entryway. Like last time, he was drawn to a framed painting on the wall over her desk. It was a sea-side landscape brought to life in swirls of blue. A few palm trees. A little boy crouched on the sand.

She stuck her head out the door. "We can order pizza if you're hungry."

Her voice died when she saw what he was up to. This time she didn't panic or try to steer his attention away from the painting. She stepped out of the bedroom, her feet and her legs bare. All he could think was that she'd denied him the pleasure of peeling off her jeans.

She stood behind him, wrapped her arms around his waist and pressed her cheek to the space between his shoulders. "I was ten when I painted that."

"Only ten?"

"Yup. My dad is from a coastal town named Saint-Marc. This is a copy of a postcard that I found tucked in one of his books."

"Have you ever been to Haiti?"

"Never," she said. "My grandfather on my mom's side is a political exile. Back in the sixties he was a little too vocal about the dictator. One night, he was arrested, but put on a plane to the Bahamas. He got off easy because his family was well connected."

Sandro guessed the ending. "He swore never to go back and forbade his children from ever returning."

"So you know how it goes."

"Oh, I know. Sounds very familiar."

Sandro perched himself at the edge of the desk. He gathered the hem of her silky top into a fist and drew her to him. "We're both connected to an island home through pretty pictures."

"It's sad when you put it that way."

"It's sad any way you put it."

She leaned into his chest and kissed his neck. The slightest touch sent rings of heat through him. "Is it tough to turn the charm on and off like that. Wherever we went people wanted a piece of you."

"It's what I signed up for. Was it tough on you?" He was already thinking long-term. Would this be a problem in the future?

"No. I always have the best time with you."

He tugged at the ties of her top and the flimsy thing fell to her waist. Her breath came quick and shallow, raising her chest, offering up her lace-clad breasts and then quickly withdrawing the offer, over and over again. Beside him on the desk was the glass of ice water. He reached for it and swiped it against a budding nipple. Angel shuddered and arched back. He caught her by the waist and drew her back to him.

"I've changed my mind." He treated the other nipple to the same torture. "I'm going to be bad."

She disentangled herself from him and stumbled back, brown skin prickled with goose bumps, wavy hair loose, liquid brown eyes blazing.

She slipped her thumbs underneath the waist of her panties and with a dip of the hips, lowered them to her ankles. She kicked them aside and fixed her gaze on him. Those haunting eyes urged him to be whoever he needed to be, good or bad, so long as he kept his word.

Angel led him to the couch. In the back of his mind, doubts were piling up. The trip to the gallery had opened up her world. This last conversation had revealed facts that he should not ignore, and yet he planned to. When he held her trembling body and sank inside her, he was thoroughly convinced that it was worth it.

I made copies.

I worked hard to re-create them.

Almost obsessively.

This is a copy.

Oh, my angel...

Sixteen

Myles sat in the quiet kitchen with his coffee mug and his recipe cards, jotting down edits to the day's menu. Sandro sat across from him at the stainless steel counter, coffee cup in hand, brooding. At this hour of the day *Diablo* was empty and calm. It was Myles's favorite part of the day. The guy fed off peace and quiet. Too bad for him it was Sandro's favorite time to visit. He'd stopped by after dropping Angel off at the gallery. As per usual, Myles brewed him a cup of coffee, spread butter on fresh baked bread, and left Sandro to eat in silence. Today was different only because the silence had gone prickly.

"If you don't tell me what's bothering you, I'm going to kick you out."

Sandro did not respond. He focused on ripping a chunk of bread to pieces, then the pieces to pieces.

"Is it that girl?" Myles asked.

Sandro wiped his hands of the crumbs with more force than the task required. "Yes."

"I like her," Myles said. "You two got a nice vibe, but you just met her. Shouldn't you chill a bit?"

"It's not a cake, man. You don't just pull it out of the oven and set it aside to chill."

Myles ran a hand through his hair and tightened the elastic that held his mane together. "You know what? You're right. I don't know crap about relationships. I'm staying out of it."

"No, you're in," Sandro said. "I've got to talk to someone."

"Then talk."

Myles tapped the butter knife on the counter to edge him on. Sandro took a breath and dove in. He told his old friend about JD's paintings, the sudden appearance of fakes on the market and Angel's infinitely small role. "I don't think she has anything to do with it."

"You don't know," Myles said. "You don't know either way. Not enough time has passed. This girl is a stranger."

"She's not."

"She is," Myles insisted. "Having said that, what does your gut tell you?"

"That she has nothing to do with this."

"Then why haven't you told her any of this? You're here, telling me this shit, and you should be telling her."

Sandro was still salty for having been thrown out of his brother's tire shop. "You're my best friend," he said. "Who else am I going to talk to?"

Myles held up his hands in the universal sign of *hold your fire!* "I was just trying to make a point, not cast doubt on the state of our union. It's strong, man."

Sandro curved forward and pressed his forehead to the

cool stainless steel countertop. "You think I should tell her."

Myles gathered his recipe cards in a stack and whacked him over the head with it. "There's nothing else you can do."

Sandro swatted his hand away. "Got any of those chocolate pastries I like?"

His friend got up from the stool. "It's called *pain chocolat*. Expand your vocabulary."

Myles had spent two years in Paris studying culinary arts and returned a snob. "Whatever. Just warm it up."

"I want you to consider something," Myles said when he returned with the warm pastry. "Miami is a cesspool of corruption. They've got this angle on you. Some unknown Cuban artist linked to a big Hollywood star. That's gold. They start a whisper campaign. Suddenly everybody wants a Valero original. They get some guy holed up in a warehouse cranking these things out. What do you think you can do about it?"

"So what are you saying? I should do nothing? Just give up?"

"Never give up, man. But you may be playing whack-a-mole. Don't you got a couple more Oscars to win?"

"I could just go public with it," Sandro said. "Let people know that they're buying fakes."

"That's a PSA some people might appreciate," Myles said. "You could pull JD's pieces out of storage and show them what the originals look like."

Every sign was pointing in this direction. "Like a gallery show."

Myles yawned. "Those things are so fucking boring. You're an artist. Can't you think of something more creative?"

Sandro nodded. Note to self: *Think of something more creative.*

"Now... about Angel."

Sandro piped up. "Yes?"

"Can't really help you there, but do you really think she's the one holed up in a warehouse pumping out these paintings? Yes or no?"

"No," Sandro said without hesitation.

"There's your answer."

Sandro folded his arms. That was his answer. Deep inside he knew that he could trust her. They'd exchanged vows, promising to keep each other's secrets and tell each other the things that mattered. He had to hold on to that.

"You've got to tell her, man," Myles said. "Otherwise, it's not fair to her."

Sandro stuffed his mouth with chocolate pastry and chewed. His quiet and wise friend was right, as always. *"Gracias, hermano."*

"Anytime."

"So, how's your mom?"

Myles shrugged. "She's got those back aches, you know."

Sandro nodded. He knew that Myles was a good son, a good friend, a good uncle to his nephew, a good cook and a good-looking guy. "Tell me something. Why are you still single?"

"Shut the hell up."

Sandro finished his pastry in two bites and wiped his mouth. Now that he'd sorted things out, he was famished. "What do I got to do to get a *croqueta* around here?"

Angel was dying at work. Alessandro had dropped her off at the gallery and would return later to take her with him to Fisher Island. In the meantime, she had nothing to do but sell postcards, T-shirts and trinkets to tourists. It was a slow day at the gallery. The desire to buy art dissipated just as soon as the Basel big tents came down. And she was fine with it. She could not focus on anything except tonight, tomorrow and the day after that. She and Alessandro would be alone for two delicious days. It might change her.

Angel was falling for him, dropping through the clouds and too blissed out to worry about the landing. She could not help but compare this affair with long-term relationships that had not felt this good, this comfortable. It had nothing to do with his celebrity status or star power. She was drawn by his vivacious spirit and generous heart. She loved the way he flirted, all his pet names for her and the jokes they shared. She loved the way he made love to her, the way he freed her so that she could make love to him without inhibitions. All this was going to end soon. She wasn't prepared. There was no way to prepare for a fatal crash.

During her lunch break, Angel looked both ways before crossing Lincoln Road to grab her usual chicken Caesar wrap and iced coffee. She found a bench in the shade. People-watching was her favorite pastime and the open-air mall was ideal for this. She watched the crowds of stylish shoppers and visitors from all over the world. When she was done eating, she took out her phone and sketched the lively scene on a drawing app.

Her phone buzzed in her hand with a FaceTime request. It was her mother. *Her mother!* Angel repressed the urge to chuck her phone into the trash. She tapped the button and her mother's broad, brown face filled the screen. Likely calling from work. Her hair was brushed neatly in a bun. She wore her usual diamond stud earrings and wine-colored lipstick to elevate her physician's white coat. Her mother had kind eyes and a broad mouth that was always quick to smile. Angel favored her father, though. He had the glamour of a sixties era crooner with wavy, slicked back hair and a trim moustache.

"Bonjour, ma fille!"

"Bonjour, Mom."

"Ah! You remember your mother. Praise God!"

"Don't start. You knew I'd be busy this week."

"Busy with what you call work, yes, I knew that. But you managed to find the time to run all over town with a movie star. Imagine my surprise!"

Oh…shit!

"It's not what it looks like, Mom. Entertaining celebrities is part of my job."

"Then get a new job."

Not this again.

"Mother, I'm a thirty-year-old woman," Angel said. "My job is my business."

It irked Angel that as she made this impassioned declaration, she sounded as peevish as a thirteen-year-old. Her behavior wasn't much better. She was lying and hiding just like when she was a teen. Angel lived her life under the dome of her parents' disapproval. Immigrants with a strict code of conduct, they'd expected their daughters to focus on their education. No parties. No proms. No dating. No boyfriends or boys as friends. In order to get around their parents' rules, and to enjoy their high school years, she and Bernadette had resorted to flat-out devious behavior, sneaking around and covering their tracks.

Alessandro had asked why she'd given up on her dreams so quickly. She'd given herself a full decade, her twenties, to achieve success. When he shared the stories of his waiter/actor days, Angel felt a pang of envy. He'd had the freedom to fail over and over again until he got it right. He didn't have exacting parents to account to. No one faulted him for the sacrifices that he was willing to make in pursuit of his dreams. Things were different for Angel.

Often her mother had bemoaned Angel's so-called lack of ambition. Once, at Thanksgiving, she'd decried the poor return on her parental investment. "All that we've done for you girls, private schools, tutors, extracurricular activities, and not one of you followed in our footsteps. Bernadette, you could have been a pediatrician." Bernadette was a nurse practitioner, which was okay, just not good enough. Say nothing about Angel's so-called "career in the arts."

Angel's definition of success was grafted onto her parents' standards. Following one's bliss was not part of the equation. At thirty she needed something to show for herself: a stable source of income, a home, a husband, a few kids on the way. As of today, she had none of those things and, frankly, didn't care. After work, she was sailing off with her movie star lover to a secluded island for a nonstop sexfest. That was the plan, and she could hardly wait. Her mother would just have to deal.

"You know what, Mom?" she said. "I'm not paid to entertain celebrities. I don't know why I said that. Alessandro is my boyfriend."

As soon as those words flew out she had wanted to recall them. He wasn't her boyfriend—no matter how good it sounded.

Thankfully, her mother didn't seem to buy it. "Uh-huh."

"Okay. So maybe he's not—"

"Angeline, *those* people don't have girlfriends or wives. *Those* people only want one thing—a good time. *They* don't care who they hurt or use."

Those words ran through her like a freight train. Alessandro certainly loved a good time. He didn't use women, though. He cleverly offered them the opportunity to use him. This way, he could walk away feeling as if he'd done a public service. *You didn't even say thank you.* Angel had known the rules from the jump. She'd signed on the dotted line.

"Mom, you don't have to worry about me."

Her mother took a sip from a Styrofoam cup. "Okay."

Angel was all too familiar with that clipped tone. "My lunch break is over. I have to go."

"Okay."

"Love you."

Her mother let out weary sigh. "Love is what's killing you, Angeline."

Seventeen

Dawn left behind nothing but pristine light. Angel shielded her eyes with a hand, but otherwise she was perfectly comfortable aboard the same boat that had transported her to paradise that first time around.

Their trip had been delayed another night. The night manager had failed to relieve Angel and she had had no choice but to pull a double shift at the gallery. She'd been too tired, too frustrated with her job, too emotionally drained from her argument with her mother and too eager to collapse into bed with Alessandro to consider packing a bag. Alessandro had picked up dinner at *Diablo* and they'd spent another night at her place, finally setting off at dawn. They were rewarded with a fresh sky and crystalline bay all to themselves.

This time the golf cart was waiting at the dock and Alessandro took the wheel. At Villa Paraiso, they bypassed security and rode straight up to the penthouse without having to check in with anyone. In the elevator, he dropped her bag and kissed her until they'd arrived at the penthouse.

"This is your home for the next forty-eight hours," he said.

"I think I'll like it here."

He gave her a tour, starting from a stark white kitchen that he planned to renovate someday, a viewing room with projector and screen, the main sitting area where they'd first met, a home office and a guest bedroom down the hall from the master suite. "This is where my niece stays when she visits."

"Will she be coming by?" Angel asked, nervous at the prospect of meeting this niece who meant so much to him.

"I'm not expecting her. She's made herself scarce these last days."

He shut the door to the guest bedroom and leaned on it. She'd caught his grim expression. "Family drama?" she asked.

"Family BS, more like it," he mumbled. "But don't worry. I won't burden you."

Angel understood all too well. She was still trying to tunnel her way out of the pile of BS her mother had dumped on her yesterday afternoon. *Love is what's killing you.*

"Family is a blessing and a curse," she said.

They looked at each other and let the silence tell the story and fill in the gaps. There was no need to get into that now.

"I envy your friendships, though," she said. "Your friends are cool."

"My friends are pretty damn great," he said. "And they like you."

She waved the comment away. "They hardly know me."

"Trust me on this—they like you," he said. "We all like you. Hell, even Maritza."

His housekeeper? She couldn't possibly!

"You're mistaken," Angel said. "I was a hot mess the last time I ran into Maritza."

"She didn't mention it," he said. "She said you were nice and polite."

Angel looked down to the oak wood floor, hoping to conceal a silly little grin. "Well, that's nice."

"Hey," he said, "I have a proposition for you."

"No!" Animated by an irrational impulse, Angel rushed to silence him with a hand pressed to his lips. "No propositions! No revenge plots! No offers for rebound sex! You like me and that's enough. I like being liked."

He pried her hand away. "That's not what I was getting at. I only meant to tell you that I've given Maritza a few days off because I wanted to be alone with you. Absolute isolation. But not having Maritza means *not* having Maritza. I don't know how to turn on our stove. So there's the issue of meals. We have options. There are several restaurants on the island. We can check those out or order in."

"Oh," she said, embarrassed at her gross overreaction to what amounted to a what-would-you-like-for-dinner-type question. "Let's order in. Definitely. Absolute isolation. I like the sound of that."

"And Angel?"

"Yes?"

"*I* like you, very, very much."

Angel went to him and took his hand. She liked being liked in general, but this was special.

"I should have said that the first night instead of inventing bullshit reasons for you to stay. All that talk about rebound sex was just…"

"What?" she asked in a whisper.

"A way to…"

"Get me naked?"

He laughed and pressed his forehead to hers. "Get you to stay."

That first night, she would have played any game he'd wanted just for the chance to be with him, get to know him, touch him, taste him. "I like you, too," she said. "Much more than I thought possible."

He burrowed his face in her neck. "What does that mean?"

Angel slid her hands under his shirt. "What does it matter now?"

"It matters if this is going to last beyond these few days."

Needing to focus, Angel stopped her wanton exploration of his skin. "You mean *us*?"

"Who else?"

Angel let out a breath. Now was the time to say the things that mattered. "At first it was just a game, a little fun. Not anymore."

He kissed her slowly and for such a long time, she melted into him. "My angel…" he whispered against her lips. "This was never a game."

"There still have to be rules."

He pulled away from her. "You and your rules!"

"They work!"

He grabbed her wrist and kissed her open palm. "Can't we just enjoy this?"

"That sounds like YOLO!"

"Not YOLO, I promise." He laughed. "I know how much you hate it."

"I should have bought that piece just to remind you."

He leaned in and kissed her. "You don't have to do that.

I remember everything about you. What you love. What you like. What you hate."

Well…she hated uncertainty. At the risk of sounding needy and clingy, Angel asked the question burning inside her. "What happens when you leave in a few days?"

"Weeks," he corrected. "I can stay through the holidays."

"Oh?" In the greater scheme of things it didn't move the dial much, but it bought them time. A new fragile leaf of hope sprouted inside her.

"Eventually, I'll be leaving for New Zealand. When the shoot wraps, there's no reason why I couldn't return here instead of LA."

"Or I could visit you in California," she proposed, so eager to meet him halfway it killed her. The need to keep him in her life bordered desperation, and wasn't that what her mother had tried to warn her against?

"If you do," he said, "I'll make each day beautiful for you. I promise."

A shiver ran through her. In no time, he had her out of her clothes. He made love to her, her back against the wall, her legs coiled around his waist. And before she knew it, Angel was saying yes to something that she did not fully grasp.

Sandro watched her sleep. A part of him worried that if he did not keep watch, she would run away again. Yesterday had been a sun-filled dream. They'd spent the entire day poolside. After a swim they shared a lounge chair. Stretched out on their backs, fingers linked, he told her about his father who'd been married when he'd met his mother and how his grandfather had stepped in to raise him when both his parents had shrugged off the responsibility. It turned out to be the best thing that could have happened to him. He grew up in a house with no rules and plenty of freedom to experiment and try on new hats. It allowed him to thrive as an artist. His grandfather, as moody and temperamental as he'd been, was Sandro's whole world as a child. His parents had all but abandoned him. Which brought him to a truth he hadn't yet fully acknowledged.

"People ask me to promote my grandfather's work and I can't do that without exposing my parents for who they were," he said. "As it is, nobody cares about my childhood. There's no way to introduce JD without the whole mess with my parents spilling out."

Beyond the biography his publicist had crafted, which stated that he was "born and raised in Miami," there wasn't much information about him out there. Nobody cared about his early life. They only wanted to know whom he was sleeping with at any given time.

She rested a hand on his chest, strengthening their connection through touch. "Where's your mother today?"

"In Pembroke Pines, married, with two grown kids," he said. "I'm the mistake she's left in her past. Although she did write when I landed my first major role."

By contrast, Angel's upbringing was exceptionally strict and proper. It seemed to Sandro that her mother was a little too involved in her affairs. Both her parents were physicians and they had done their best to stifle her creativity. They considered her MFA degree a waste of time and money. They disapproved of her "bohemian" lifestyle. He guessed that she'd given up on her art in large part because of familial pressure. When he tried to get her to admit it, she sat up on her knees and begged him to change the subject.

He obliged by bringing up Gallery Six. Understandably, she didn't want to talk about work. He dropped that topic, too. He couldn't avoid it for too long. He had to tell her that the painting she'd sold him was a fake; he owed her that much. He remembered how she'd reacted when he'd withheld his grandfather's identity. How much worse was this?

The news would affect her in more ways than one. She'd have to come to terms with the fact that her employer was dealing fakes, either knowingly or unknowingly. Angel would have some choices to make. Would she ignore the facts and keep her job? Would she confront Paloma and potentially lose her job? He wasn't comfortable with either option. For sure, he'd like her less if she didn't take this seriously. And yet, he didn't want her to lose her job because of him.

There was a lot to consider. He couldn't just spring the news on her. After the week she'd had, it would be cruel to dump it on her now. She needed this reprieve. He needed this time with her, untainted and untouched by the outside world.

Last night, they'd ordered gourmet pizza, ate dinner at the kitchen island, silenced their phones and went to bed fairly early. She stirred beside him now.

He rolled over to her, drew her into a spoon. His palm found the curve of her breast. Their breathing synched. A moment later, she lifted her head off the pillow and her whole body went stiff.

"What's the matter?" he asked.

"Nothing," she said. "I'm fine."

Fine was code for *I'm freaking out*. He knew that much.

"Want to run away again?"

"Don't be ridiculous!" She set her head back down but did not relax.

"Something is bothering you." He kissed her neck and her shoulder muscles knotted up. "You're tense."

She turned around in his arms and faced him, the tips of their noses touching. "This feels good."

"And that's bad?"

"It feels too good."

"No such thing as *too good*, Angel," he murmured sleepily.

She broke away from him and sat up, drawing the sheets over her chest, which was completely unnecessary. It was still dark; he could make out only the lines of her body.

"This feels too good for what it is," she said. "Does that make sense?"

So early in the morning, nothing made sense. "What time is it?"

"Six. I always wake up at six."

"Always?" he asked, groggy.

"Always."

"Well, not today. Come to me." He reached for her and pulled her deeper into their cocoon, drawing the heavy blanket around them. It didn't solve the real problem. She was still tense. He kissed her forehead and smoothed back her hair. "You're afraid of getting hurt again. Is that it?"

"Of course I am!" she exclaimed. "What about you? I could hurt you. Or don't you think that's possible?"

It was not only possible; it was highly probable. What was she going to do when he left? Sit around and wait? "Angel, you could tear me to shreds, and I'd take it," he said. "Notice I'm not the one who wants to bolt."

She closed her eyes. The flutter of her lashes tickled his chin. "Sorry. I like to panic first thing in the morning."

Maybe it was time that he made his wants clear. "I want to take the risk," he said. "I want to be the man in your life, and in your bed. I want to wake up beside you whenever I can. And I want to be good to you."

"Good?" she said. "In what way?"

"In any way you'll let me, my angel."

He couldn't bulldoze his way into her life, particularly

because he was not in a position to promise the usual things: Friday nights at the movies, Saturday night dinner dates and Sunday picnics at the park—or whatever it was people in love were doing these days.

Love. Was that what this was?

She crawled on top of him, sat up and pinned him down between her thighs, pushing away sheets, dismantling the cocoon. In the glow of the thin rays of light sneaking into the room, she was magnificent. Waves of hair framed her face. The smooth lines of her body silhouetted against the light.

"Do you panic every morning?"

"Like clockwork."

"Damn."

"It'll pass," she said. "Physical activity helps."

Well...he was her chew toy.

"Have at it," he said.

Their gazes held and she bent forward to kiss him. Before their lips touched, she whispered that she wanted to be good to him, too.

GOLDEN GLOBES NOMINATIONS

Best Performance by an Actor in a Supporting Role in a Series, Limited Series or Motion Picture Made for Television

Brad Baxter, *The Hit Job*
Alessandro Cardenas, *Black Market*
Zach Harris, *The Agency*
Nicholas Jones, *Good Vibes Only*
Robert West, *Moving Target*

Eighteen

No matter what, Angel could not snuff out a looming sense of doom. It was ridiculous. Everything was perfect. Swimming all day, talking all afternoon, a glass of wine at sunset, sketching by the pool while her lover studied lines, gourmet pizza for dinner delivered to their door— Angel had never had a more perfect day. Waking up beside Alessandro was a gift tailor-made for her. And yet she could not relax. The tension just wouldn't ease up. *I want to enjoy this. Why can't I?*

She blamed her mother. She'd poisoned her mind.

Or was it Chris?

And if no one was to blame, then what was wrong with *her*? Couldn't she be happy for a while?

They'd made love in the early morning and fallen back asleep. The house was peaceful, but her thoughts raged. Then it happened: the equivalent of a five-star alarm.

Alessandro's mobile phone started buzzing and chiming like a vengeful bumblebee, so much so it spun off the nightstand landing onto the wood floor with a thud. Somewhere in the distance a landline telephone started ringing nonstop. Angel shot upright, heart pounding. "What is it? What's going on?"

Alessandro, unruffled as always, rolled over and scooped his phone off the floor. He tapped the screen and scrolled through his messages and alerts. A lazy grin spread across his face. "Holy shit! I got a Golden Globe nom."

Was that all? Angel fell back against the pillows, relief rushing through her. She'd nearly had a stroke, there! She shoved her dark thoughts to the back of her mind and offered him a bright smile. "Congratulations! That's exciting!"

"Thanks." He chucked the phone and pounced on her. He was most handsome in the morning, scruffy and disheveled. She did not take this for granted. "Be my date, babe."

"For what?"

"The Globes."

Wow! It wasn't the prospect of walking the red carpet that excited her. Actually, she might turn that down. The award shows typically aired in February. Alessandro was making plans for several months out. That realization set off pinwheels of joy.

"I have a ball gown in the back of my closet," she said. "It'll do."

"No…" His hands explored her naked body under the sheets. "I like you in those light silky dresses."

"You do?"

"Oh, yes…" He kissed her neck and the rough skin of his cheek scraped the tender skin just below her ear. "The ones with the thin straps… It drives me crazy."

"Will you wear a blue suit?" she asked. "Like the blue Tom Ford you wore to the Emmys?"

He kissed the tip of her nose. "That was Armani, but sure, whatever you like."

"May I choose the tie?"

"May I tie you to the bed post with it afterward?"

"Or maybe I'll tie you."

"I knew it." He dipped his head and kissed the hollow of her neck. "You're no angel, and I love it."

Angel broke out in laughter. The dark clouds that crowded her mind quickly dissipated.

"Come on!" he said, pulling away. "Let's celebrate."

"With champagne?"

"Overrated," he replied. "With coffee."

She slipped on a T-shirt. He pulled on a pair of board shorts. They puttered barefoot down the hall to the bright, immaculate kitchen. Angel wandered over to the picture window. She stretched and did a few rounds of sun salutations while Alessandro proceeded to brew coffee. Essentially he shoved a pod into a fancy machine. Nevertheless, she still felt like the most cared for and pampered woman in the world.

"What got you nominated?" she asked, gliding from downward dog to upward dog. The aroma of coffee filled the kitchen.

"*Black Market*, the FastFlix miniseries."

"Oh, no! I haven't seen it!"

He pulled a milk frother from a drawer. "What?"

"Sorry! I don't have that streaming app!"

She wasn't the least sorry. Angel had no intention of signing up for another streaming service. Enough was enough!

He held up the frother. "My ego is as fragile as you'd expect, and I hate to say it—I'm hurt."

"Awww!" She rushed over to hug him. "I love your work. You know that."

He leaned into her. "Go on. Stroke my ego."

"Sure," Angel said, pushing him away. "But first, coffee."

He retrieved a glass bottle of milk from the refrigerator. "Myles taught me how to make a decent cappuccino."

"Then that's what I'll have."

"One cappuccino coming up."

She watched as he methodically poured frothy milk into two coffee mugs and handed her one. Then he stepped out of the kitchen to return his agent's calls. Angel searched around for a television remote and switched on the flat screen mounted on the wall in the breakfast nook. She took her coffee to the marble-top table and flipped through the channels. The local TV networks might replay the award nominations, if only to celebrate their local boy. Channel 3, Channel 6, Channel 7, Channel 10...and wait... A headline grabbed her attention.

Days after Art Basel, allegations of fraud rattle the art market.

The news anchor, a young man who'd risen in visibility thanks to his coverage of the last hurricane, promised more details after the commercial break. Angel sipped her coffee, which was delicious, and waited. Which gallery had messed up this time? Art dealers never learned. Greed was at the rotting core of the art market; that was the unvarnished truth. It filtered every transaction with suspicion. Just last year, one of the oldest, most prestigious galleries in North America had to shut down when it was caught peddling a fake Rothko. Angel had absolutely no sympathy for...

"FBI raids Miami Beach art gallery, a Lincoln Road staple for over two decades...

"Gallery Six, named after the six daughters of Florida billionaire Lawrence Saxton, was raided early today. The feds seized computers and records. At the heart of the scandal is Paloma Gentry aka Paula Claire Gentry, arrested at dawn under allegations of money laundering. Ms. Gentry joined the gallery in 2012."

Nineteen

"What did I tell you?" Leslie said. "That award is as good as yours!"

"Calm down. It's an honor to be nominated."

"That's BS and you know it!" Leslie scoffed. "Plus the field is weak. I like your chances."

"Whether you win or not, we should capitalize on the pre-award show craze." This was Cameron, Sandro's publicist. Leslie had conferenced her into the call. The women worked as a tag team. "I'd like you to post a candid photo or a short video, maybe a TikTok, of your reaction to the news. You know the drill."

"I know the drill."

"I'll line up interviews and keep you posted," she said. "You may want to consider coming home now."

Sandro's mood fell flat. "Is that necessary?"

"Uh, yeah!" Cameron said. "We'll want you to do the late-night talk show circuit and maybe even *The Talk* or

The View. It might be a good idea to start with the New York circuit since you're on the East Coast."

"Don't sign me up for anything yet. Give me a couple of days."

"First you didn't want time off and now you're begging for more time?" Leslie intervened. "You're no better than my kids."

The sound of breaking glass reached him from the kitchen. Had Angel hurt herself? "Ladies, I gotta go."

"What did I say?" Leslie said. "Just like my kids."

Sandro rushed into the kitchen. Angel was at the round table near the window. Her cup was shattered on the floor, a puddle spread across the tile. Angel hadn't budged. She sat very still, staring at the television screen. Nothing special was on, just an auto insurance commercial. Sandro had to wonder if she was losing her mind.

"Angel!" He sidestepped the mess. "Babe, are you okay?"

She turned to him, blinking, snapping out of whatever trance she'd been in. She stood and opened wide eyes to the mess at her feet. "Oh, God! Look at this! Sorry!"

Sandro pressed a hand to her forehead. "Look at *me*. What's going on?"

"I have to go."

"What?"

"I have to go. I'm so sorry, but I have to go."

She wiggled free from him and headed out of the kitchen. He chased after her, genuinely panicked. "Angel, talk to me. Where are you going?"

She burst into the bedroom and whirled around, searching for articles of clothing. "I have to get back to Miami. You have to help me get off this island."

"Why?" he demanded.

"It's crazy!" She got down on her hands and knees to

reach for a pair of sandals under the bed. He recalled that she'd kicked them off on the morning of her arrival and that's where they'd landed. "The FBI raided the gallery!"

Sandro snapped out of his own trance. "What are you talking about?"

She stood and faced him. "Paloma was arrested this morning!"

"Shit!"

"I have to go back."

"To do what? Bail her out?"

"No! Be serious."

She darted into the bathroom and started shoving mini bottles into her zipped pouch. She paused only to gather and secure her hair into a ponytail. The blond, face-framing wisps had long faded. She looked exactly as she had the day they'd first met. Glowing brown skin. Messy hair. Guarded expression. Like that first day, she wore white. Except this time she had on one of his many cotton T-shirts.

He crowded the door. "I am serious. What do you expect to do for them?"

She grabbed her toothbrush. She was intent on leaving and Sandro felt the first stirs of panic.

"It's the gallery," she said. "It's my job. I have to find out what's going on. Do I even have a job anymore? Don't you think I should find out?"

"No. I think you should stay away from those criminals."

She zipped the pouch shut, pushed past him and shoved it into her travel bag open at the foot of the bed. "Sandro, this is bad. This is really bad. Last year one of the biggest galleries in New York shut when it was caught selling fakes."

"All the more reason for you to stay away."

"Here's the thing," she said, folding a bathing suit into the bag. "I've worked with these people. Paloma is a lot of things, but she's not a criminal. This has to be a mistake."

Sandro couldn't take it anymore. "There's no mistake."

She went still for the first time since he'd found her at the kitchen table. Brows drawn, she turned to him. "How are you so sure?"

Oh, Angel.

Sandro felt sick. He'd been waiting for the perfect time to come clean. The time was now and it was far from perfect. One thing was certain: Angel would not forgive him.

Moments later, Angel hollered at the top of her lungs. "You let me sell you a *fake* painting!"

The look in those clear brown eyes told him just how betrayed she felt.

"I didn't know it was fake. I had my suspicions, but I didn't know for sure."

"The only reason you bought it is because you suspected it was fake!"

"Suspected, yes," he said. "I had no proof."

"But then you had proof and you *still* didn't tell me." She covered her eyes with her hands. "I can't believe it. All this was going on and you didn't tell me."

"I wanted to catch the people involved without involving you. You worked for them. I couldn't be sure—"

"Of my involvement?"

"No!" he protested. "Let's just say, the less you knew the better."

"We were sleeping together!"

"We *are* sleeping together. Don't go putting us in the past tense."

"Here I thought we were growing close."

"We *are* close."

Sandro hated himself for how meek and desperate he sounded. He could have told her, but their relationship had been only days old. It would have shattered this fragile thing between them.

He went over to where she stood at the foot of the bed. "I only ever wanted to shield you from all this."

"Shield me? Don't you think it would have been smarter to warn me about the possible risks of working in a den of thieves? You knew I was trying to get my career on track. I could have gotten out before the scandal broke."

She had a point there. "I didn't think—"

"No, you didn't!"

"Angel, I'm sorry. This whole thing is one big cluster..."

Angel wasn't listening to him. She bit into her lower lip in that way she did whenever deep in thought. "That first night? Were you trying to keep me around to pump information out of me?"

Emotion rumbled through him and left him trembling. "Don't do that," he said through clenched teeth. "Don't make that first time into something ugly. If I'd wanted information, I would've asked straight up."

That night, he hadn't wanted to talk about the painting at all.

"Tell me the truth," she said. "Part of you suspected that I played a role in this."

"No. Never."

"Not even when I showed up at your house with a forged painting?"

Sandro dug his hands in his pockets, unbothered. "Not even."

She took a step closer, wielding a forefinger like a sword. "Lie to me now and I'll never trust you again."

In an odd way, the threatening statement gave him hope. He wouldn't lose her over this. It wouldn't break them.

"The thought crossed my mind once."

She lowered her hands to her hips, looking formidable. "When was that?"

"When we went to Papaya, and you told me how you taught yourself to paint."

She crinkled her nose. "I don't follow."

"You copied the paintings in your parents' collection. You reproduced them."

"Oh, God." She folded over and fell onto the bed, looking gutted. "That night we'd shared so much. I opened up to you."

"It was a passing thought. It never sank in."

"I told you about my family, my grandfather, my dad's hometown…" She mumbled the words, speaking mostly to herself.

Fear kicked him in the gut. This could very well break them. "I was confused. That's all."

"We made love."

He joined her on the bed, sitting beside her. It was time to come clean and still he kept one more thing from her. He had fallen in love with her that night.

"Stay," he said. "We can talk this through."

"We had rules, Alessandro," she said. "We promised to tell each other the things that mattered. Didn't you think this mattered?"

This time her words were sharp and clear. It was his turn to ramble. "I did. I didn't know. I…"

Her phone blinked on the bedside table, catching her

attention. Ignoring him, she got up to retrieve it and stared at the screen before raising it to her ear. "Hello."

Sandro heard the muffled sounds of a man's voice. Angel said, "I'll be there." She lowered the phone and turned to him. "I can't stay. The FBI wants to question me."

Twenty

Clearing her name with the FBI did not matter as much as clearing her name with Alessandro. Angel sat stone-faced through the interview and tossed out perfunctory answers to their questions. She had consented mainly to avoid hiring an attorney and because she had nothing to hide—two of the worst reasons to risk self-incrimination, that was for sure. When she stepped out of the nondescript building in Downtown Miami, there he was, still waiting, two hours later.

He wore his cap, sunglasses and the plain clothes that allowed him to blend in. When he hugged her she did not pull away. Angel needed to be held. She was emotion-ally drained.

"If they try to pin this on you, I'll hire a team of law-yers. You are not taking the fall for those people."

She pulled away and looked up at his face, his strong

features lined with concern. "How do you know that I'm not one of those people?"

"Angel…"

She was serious. How could he ever really trust her? It was upon her to clear her name. She could tell he was anxious to sweep the dirty business under a rug and move past it. But that was impossible.

Angel waited until they were in the car before she spoke. "They don't care about forgeries."

Alessandro pressed the ignition button. "I'm not surprised. No one does."

"They only wanted to know about Paloma's sales roster, names of clients, etc."

"What do you think is going on there?"

"I don't know." Angel looked at his sharp profile as he eased the car into traffic and wished she wasn't so head over heels for him. "That doesn't help you, though."

"Help with what?"

"Finding the person who forged your grandfather's paintings."

"My brother and Myles both want me to let that go, so maybe I should."

"No," Angel said, a stubborn determination taking hold in her. "I want to help you figure this out."

"No," he said, sounding just as stubborn. "You want to prove something to me. And I don't want you to prove anything."

"Head north on 95," she said, as they approached the junction.

"Why?" he asked. "Don't you want to go home?"

"There's someone we need to speak to first."

His grip on the wheel tightened. "Who?"

"Justine Carr."

* * *

Justine lived in a quiet neighborhood in North Miami. Her house was a plain ranch-style home, the kind that cropped up everywhere back in the seventies. At first glance, it did not look like much, a flat roof and a brick facade painted white. When Justine opened for them, holding the door wide, Angel got a view straight through the house to the backyard and noted that it bordered onto a canal complete with dock.

Justine did not look like her clever self, with her corn-yellow hair in a messy bun and her right foot trapped in an orthopedic boot. Her weary blue gaze slid from Angel to Alessandro. Angel felt like the pet cat that had brought a dead rat into the house.

"I don't want to get mixed up in any family drama," she said.

"Well, hello to you, too," Angel replied, wondering what exactly she meant by that.

"Alessandro Cardenas," Justine said, quite obviously sizing him up. "We meet at last."

Alessandro had kept his distance, casting a look around as if he did not trust the neighborhood. Dressed as he was, he looked as if he were playing the role of her bodyguard.

"We spoke on the phone once," he said.

"Simpler times," she said dryly, then stepped aside to let them in. "You're lucky you found me. I just got back from Costco."

She said this as if it were an ordinary day and her list of mundane errands was all that mattered. "That's cool," Angel replied. "I just came back from an FBI interrogation."

Justine rolled her eyes. "Those fools! I told them you had nothing to do with anything."

"They didn't take your word for it," Angel said. "Thanks anyway."

Instead of inviting them into her living room, she led them past her kitchen, a gleaming granite and stainless steel box, straight to the yard where a few rattan chairs were set up around a fire pit. She led them past those, too, and straight to the dock where a cooler and a few throw pillows were stacked. The water that drifted through the canal was a particular shade of blue green. Cobalt green, if sold by the tube at the art supply store.

"What are we drinking?"

It wasn't yet lunchtime. "I…ugh…water?"

That eye roll again. "After the morning you had? They must have gone soft with you. They had me held up for five hours yesterday."

Angel sank down onto the splintered wood dock, allowing her legs to hang over the edge. She grabbed Alessandro by the hem of his T-shirt and drew him down beside her. He draped a protective arm over her shoulders. Angel's mood shifted like sand. As angry and resentful as she was with him, she was still more comfortable with him than any man she'd ever dated. It was as if life was playing a cruel joke.

"Look at you two all cozy," Justine said. "I must have done you a favor of a lifetime when I got hit by that puny car."

She flipped open the cooler and rummaged through the ice for a chilled can of beer from a local brewery. Angel recognized the blue 305 logo. Alessandro raised a hand and she tossed the can to him. He cracked it open.

Everyone was having a swell time.

Angel got back to business. "I need another favor."

"Here!" She tossed Angel a can. "Have a beer instead."

Had Justine always been this wily? Yes, she had.

Using a wood post as support, she slid down next to them and propped her booted foot onto the stack of pillows. Mimicking Alessandro, she cracked open her can.

"Yeah… Paloma screwed us over with those so-called private sales of hers," she said.

Angel set the can down. "What do you know about it?"

"She helped some really sketchy characters to buy and sell art at outrageous prices as a way for money to exchange hands. She got kickbacks for her trouble. Did you see any of that kickback money?"

"No," Angel said. "Did you?"

"No." Justine took a sip of beer. "You know what really bothers me? Those crooks likely tossed those paintings into a ditch when they were done. They didn't care."

A seagull swooped low and flew off. Justine cared about art; Angel knew that much. A graduate of Sotheby's, she was serious about her work and, therefore, excelled.

"Now what am I going to do?" she said. "I was Miss Gallery Six. Everybody knew me from the East Coast to the West as Miss Gallery Six. Now Gallery Six is closed and I'm screwed."

Alessandro had some advice. "Move to a new city. Start over."

Angel disagreed. Moving to LA might have worked out for him, but her move to Miami was a disaster from start to finish.

"I'm not moving anywhere," Justine said. "This house is home. I've put everything I have into it. I'm going to sit here, drink my beer, feed the alligators and wave to my neighbors as they sail by."

Justine…always so dramatic! "No one ever called the shop asking to speak with Miss Gallery Six. Your clients knew you by name and would only work with you. Reach out and tell them you're flying solo, freelancing. Next thing you'll know, you're back on the scene."

"I guess..." A little smiled teased at the corners of Justine's mouth. "And what about you, little one?"

"Me? I guess I'll move back home."

"Why?"

Justine and Alessandro had shouted the one-word question in unison. They were both glaring at her. All Angel could think to say was "Because!" She might not be Miss Gallery Six, but how could she ever escape it now?

"Don't let your stint at the gallery shape your life. You were nothing but the salesgirl."

"Gee, thanks!" Angel reached for her can of beer and cracked it open. It was lunchtime somewhere.

"I'm serious! When anyone asks you say that you were just the salesgirl, hadn't even worked there a year. You're young and you're pretty and no one will care."

"I'm not that young!" Angel protested.

Justine treated her to yet another epic eye roll. "Just do me a favor," she said. "Do something you really love. You're not really suited at pushing art."

"I'm not really suited at anything!" Angel said, annoyed.

Alessandro was quick to console her. "That's not true!"

"It is true!"

Angel looked up to the sky, at a cluster of clouds in the shape of a continent. She had a lot to figure out, but now wasn't the time. Next to her, Alessandro's body was tight and tense. He must be so confused as to what they were actually doing here, drinking beer on a dock with her former colleague, but he was playing along. She lowered a hand to his thigh and he immediately covered it with one of his own.

They all fell silent for a while, watching the dark blue-green water flow through the canal. It felt good to sit and enjoy the quiet.

Justine stretched her arms over her head. Eyeing them, she said, "I know why you're here and I'm going to help you out."

Angel lit up. "You are?"

"Yup." She took a long sip from her can. "This shitty year is almost over. I should do one kind thing to set things up for next year."

That wasn't how it worked, generally, but Angel was game.

Justine tilted to one side to better catch Alessandro's eyes. "Your niece is selling your granddad's paintings."

If Alessandro hadn't been holding her hand, Angel might have toppled into the canal. His niece, his *beloved* niece, was peddling fake artwork? No, that's not what Justine had said. His beloved niece was selling his grandfather's art. It was possible Justine didn't know that the paintings were fakes. If that were the case, she hoped Alessandro wouldn't say anything to give it away. After all, the less anyone knew, the better.

Alessandro had gone very still. He looked struck, but not surprised. When he slipped off his sunglasses to better meet Justine's gaze, Angel noted that his hand trembled a bit. His voice, though, was even. "Where did she get these paintings from? Do you know?"

"I never asked," Justine replied. "Figured she plucked them off the walls of the family compound. My guess is that she needed the money. Sadly, I see this sort of thing everyday. She dropped your name quite a lot, in case I'd missed the connection."

Angel ran her hand along Alessandro's arm. His jaw was tight and his shoulders bunched up with tension. She felt terrible, understanding for the first time the magnitude of pressure that he'd been under. Alessandro had been working alone to find answers, with no one to rely on but himself. His brother and his best friend had advised him to give up. To discover that his niece, the one person he seemed to cherish, had forged his grandfather's work and used his name to sell it, well…it made her gripes seem like small, shriveled potatoes.

Alessandro's reaction impressed her. He politely thanked Justine for the information and got up on his feet. She blinked up at him towering over her, solid and stable, even after such a brutal blow. She saw him, not through the screen of his fame and fortune, but the rose-tinted lens of any woman in love with any man. He extended a hand and those shifting sands of emotions settled into solid ground. She took his hand and let him lift her up.

Angel helped Justine to her feet and she walked them to her door. "Come back in happier times," she said. "I'll fire up the grill."

Some neighbors had gathered on the sidewalk across the street to check out the gleaming sports car in Justine's driveway. A woman pointed when she recognized Alessandro. They quickly ducked into the car before anyone pulled out a cell phone camera. They drove off in silence. Alessandro kept his eyes on the road, his jaw tight. From time to time, he would run a palm over his rugged cheek. Very soon, a thick, oppressive silence filled the car. It was a relief when, at the press of a button, he lowered the top.

They cruised along Rickenbacker Causeway. He was driving her home, which was what she'd wanted, or so she'd thought. The mystery was solved. The gallery was closed and she had no plans to bail out Paloma from federal custody, if she hadn't made bail already. There wasn't anything for her to do at home except wallow. Yet she'd made such a scene this morning, he was probably reluctant to invite her back. Would he ever invite her back?

They were about to zip past the beach when Alessandro hooked a sharp right, pulling into the public parking lot. He found a spot facing the water, parked and cut off the engine. Angel held her breath, waiting for his next move. He leaned forward and pressed his forehead to the steering wheel and let out a long breath. Her heart ached for him.

"I wanted to tell you, Angel," he said, his voice raw. "I thought I had time. I wanted us to have those days together. Just you and me. Happy. I thought I had time." He paused and exhaled. "I wasn't trying to mislead you. Tell me you won't shut the door on us."

Angel was stunned. After all that he'd just learned, he was *still* focused on her. She released her resentment to the wind. Maybe it was a mistake to trust him again, but it was a mistake she just might have to make.

She snapped off her seatbelt and lunged at him. "Don't worry about any of that."

He cradled her to his chest and, for a while, the rolling sounds of the surf rocked them both.

"You have so much to deal with," she said. "What are you going to do?"

"I'm going to find Sabina and confront her. Let her know that I know what she's up to and that it better stop."

"How will you get your money back?" she asked.

He laughed and it rolled right through her. "Forget the money. She can keep it. Consider it a lifetime of birthday and Christmas gifts wrapped in one."

"Do you want me to go with you when you confront her?"

"No, my angel," he said. "I'm taking you home. I have to do this myself."

"Okay," she said, nestling closer to him. "Take me home, but first give me a minute."

She wanted this time with him.

Twenty-One

On the morning of JD's funeral, Sandro and Eddy had met in their grandfather's art studio, a shed thrown up in the yard of his house without any care for zoning laws or local regulations. The topic of the meeting was money. Funeral expenses had quickly accrued. Even the most modest of services cost money. Previously, they'd decided to split the costs. That morning, Eddy suggested Sandro sell JD's paintings, art supplies and furniture to raise money.

Sandro didn't follow his logic. "Hold a garage sale or something?"

"A garage sale! Bingo!"

"If we sold everything, we probably wouldn't raise more than $500 and that wouldn't put a dent in it."

JD didn't have many prize possessions to offload. The furniture was old and broken and the house in the Little River neighborhood was a rental. He'd lived in it for years and the homeowners, who wanted only a stable renter, had overlooked JD's many breaches to the lease, the least of which was the art studio shed. He owned a truck and a boat that he took out on weekends and holidays. Sandro noticed that Eddy hadn't mentioned selling those big-ticket items.

"I know you want the boat, but if we sold the Ford it would cover everything."

Eddy's face had crumbled. "I have plans for the truck."

"I have plans for the paintings."

"Like what?" Eddy snapped.

"It's personal. I don't expect you to understand."

Sandro would never forget the flash of anger in his brother's eyes and his own gut reaction to it. It didn't help that Eddy had grown into the spitting image of the father they'd both lost, milky white skin, hawk nose and thinning black hair. It was getting tough for Sandro to compartmentalize his feelings for the two men. He was beginning to resent them both.

"I'm opening a business soon. That truck will help."

"The boat is yours," Sandro said. "That's what JD wanted. The truck is for sale. If you want to buy it at a reduced price, we can talk about that."

The discussion had ended there. It was time to head out to the cemetery for the simple graveside ceremony. Afterward, family and friends gathered at the house. The neighbors brought over tons of food. Some of the guys were huddled in the yard, drinking and smoking. Eddy flicked his lit cigarette and fire tore through the shed.

Sandro left Angel with the promise that he'd return later that night. As soon as he pulled out of the gates of the rental community, he got Sabina on the phone.

Her voice spilled out of the car speakers. "Congratulations on the Golden Globe nomination, Tío!"

Christ! That seemed like a decade ago.

"Thanks," he said. "Listen, I need to see you."

"Um… How about a brunch on Sunday?"

"No," he said. *Ahora mismo.*

"Really?"

"Yes."

"Is it urgent?" she said. "I'm with my boyfriend."

"Ask him to give you ten minutes. It won't take long."

She rattled off a Miami Beach address. Sandro was not interested in creating a stir, pulling up in the flashy sports car. He got Gus on the phone and made arrangements to switch vehicles. A half hour later, he was riding Gus's motorcycle. The helmet worked as the perfect barrier between him and the world.

When he arrived at the given address, Sabina was pacing the sidewalk before a sunny three-story art deco building. She looked lovely, as always, in a cherry-red sundress, glossy chestnut hair straight down her back and eyes hidden behind round sunglasses. She pointed to the motorcycle and smirked. "New toy?"

"A loaner."

"Nice," she said in a breath. "Tío, I'd like to invite you up but…"

Was she kidding? Hot, thirsty and patience running thin, he wasn't up for this. "I don't care where we go, but we can't stay here. We have to speak in private."

Sabina folded her arms across her chest and took a rigid stance. "What's this all about?"

Sandro had no doubt that she knew exactly what this was all about, which explained the stalling tactics. "I'm not getting into it on the sidewalk."

"Hmm…follow me."

She led him up two flights of narrow stairs and down a hall to a black door marked APT A in gold art deco font. Sabina unlocked the door and ushered him inside. The apartment was very much a guy's place. The furniture consisted of glass-top tables and leather seating. "Who's the boyfriend?"

No answer.

"Will I get to meet him?"

"He stepped out."

"So…why couldn't I come up?"

Her cheeks brightened. "He'll be back soon, and you know…"

He didn't know. "Doesn't he know we're related?"

She crossed the room and plopped down on a black leather ottoman. "Just tell me what's so important."

Her harsh tone hurt him. Was he kidding himself for hoping they could resolve this and move on? In reality, his bond with his niece had frayed long ago. Gone were the days when they hung out together, caught a movie and lunch. Even when she stayed on Fisher Island, it was to hang out with the daughter of the trust fund manager who lived in the building.

Sandro dropped his helmet on a bench under a shuttered window. His eye caught a framed painting hanging over a media console with a turntable and a stack of vinyl records. It was a field of sunflowers, faces upturned to the sky, each flower distinct from the other in that distinct JD style.

"You painted that, didn't you?"

"It's a hobby," she said with a slight shrug.

Sandro lowered his head and laughed. "I should have known it was you. The truth was glaring at me the whole time. I was blinded by my love for you, my affection for you…"

Sabina balled her hands into fists. She had ditched her sunglasses when they entered the apartment and she looked young and lost.

"Why?" he asked. "You're so talented. Why use me to sell JD's paintings? You could have had a career of your own."

Sabina shook her head as if she couldn't believe how dense he was. "No one is going to pay top dollar for some Instagrammer's artwork, no matter who they're related to."

"And they'll pay top dollar for the work of a long-dead unknown?"

"Do you want to know why I'm so good at what I do?" His answer would have been no, but she continued. "Social media content is only as good as the story it tells."

Sandro pulled a chair from the dining table and sat facing her. As it so happened, he was in the storytelling business. "If you've got a good story, I'm dying to hear it."

Sabina sat up a little straighter to make up for the inches in height she lacked. It killed him that she saw in him an adversary even though he had come to confront her.

"How does this sound?" she said. "Picture a grandfather, a political exile, who supports his grandchild by peddling paintings of his childhood memories in Cuba. Then lo and behold, that grandchild grows up to be American royalty, a movie star with an Oscar. He lives in Hollywood and his face is on billboards and covers of magazines. It's the goddamn American Dream and people will pay top dollar for it. Do you get it, Tío? It's not the paintings people pay for. It's the mystique."

He had to admit, she told a damn good story. Too bad it was to rip people off. "If you needed money—"

"I don't need money," she said imperiously. "I am doing very well. I did it for Dad."

"What?" Had Eddy put her up to this?

"I don't know if you noticed that last time you rolled through," Sabina said, "but he's not exactly rolling in money up there. He mortgaged his house to finance the shop and he was going to lose both. I came up with the scheme, so don't go blaming him."

Sandro covered his face with a hand, trying to digest it all. The shop had been nearly empty when he'd stopped by, but he'd figured it was a low point in the day. Another thing leaped at him from that day, Eddy's certainty that he would never catch the forger. Had he known that his love for his niece would blind him to the truth?

"Why not come to me? I could've helped out." Just asking him for the money was a far less complicated plan than the one she'd concocted.

"Dad doesn't want your money!"

"Why the hell not?"

"Because you're not the son who should have made it," Sabina said. "I know this sounds terrible, but I might as well tell you the whole truth since you're sitting here. You are the kid that *my* grandfather conceived with some girl he picked up at a bar and here you are today, a movie star! It's eating Dad up inside. It's stupid and it's petty. I don't feel that way. I love you a lot. But he's my father. I had to find a way to help him. Please don't hate me for it."

Sandro hated himself for what he was going to say next. "How much does he need to get out of this?"

Her gaze dropped. "I don't know."

"Give me a number," he growled.

"About eighty grand."

"I'll see what I can do."

She jumped to her feet. "He won't take money from you!"

"But he'll take it from you," Sandro said. "I got a crash lesson on money laundering today and this is what we're going to do. I'll give you the cash, you'll give it to him, and that will be the end of it."

She settled back down. "That might work. I'll tell him I sold more paintings."

"About that," Sandro said. "The paint you've been using wasn't available for commercial use back in the day. At any time any buyer can discover they've been duped. Good thing Gallery Six was raided this morning and the FBI arrested the manager. The blame will likely fall on her. But if any other Valero paintings pop up on the market, I'll know about it. Next time, I won't be this understanding."

Sabina grew pale. "It won't happen again," she said. "I've been sick about it. Why do you think I've been avoiding you?"

Eddy, fucking Eddy... How could he have put his daughter in such a terrible position? After JD's death, Sandro had felt obligated to keep his dwindling family together. He was free of that burden now. Eddy could take the money and go to hell. He hoped it would buy Sabina her freedom. If it didn't, she'd have to fight for it herself. She was, after all, a multitalented young woman. She could handle herself.

Twenty-Two

Angel filled the tub, dropped in a lavender-scented bath bomb, and slipped on a bunny-eared headband. No news from Alessandro. No need to mope around. Initiate full-code #selfcaresunday on a Wednesday! She slathered on a thick coat of green moisturizing mask that promised to tighten and brighten with the use of sea algae. For a split second she wondered whether Chris would approve. And then it hit her.

Oh, God…it's only Wednesday.

Alessandro Cardenas had entered her life exactly one week ago. One week! She had aged during that week. She'd likely sprouted gray hairs; if she searched, she would find some. Angel sank onto the Lucite vanity bench that matched her bathroom's faded 1980s glamour, as did most of the apartment, which kept the rent relatively cheap. One week to turn her life upside down. Now, granted, he wasn't responsible for Paloma's shady shit. It wasn't his fault that she'd stayed on at a job that did not fulfill her, ignoring her own instincts on which path to take. She couldn't blame him that she had failed to define success for herself, letting her mother's voice stoke her fears of failure—as if failing was the worst thing that could happen in the course of a life. But he'd come at a time when the dormant volcano had erupted.

Alessandro's presence had shone a great bright light in the dark corners of her life. Things that she'd wanted to sweep up under the rug—her dependence on Chris, her lack of focus on her future, her irrational fear of failure and her need to feel secure. She had to clean up her act. She could fly without a safety net. She could tell her mother, and her sister, too, for that matter, to back off, and not lose her cool—without losing anything, really. She could do it and move forward. If she failed, she failed. She was still young enough to make mistakes. Life didn't end at thirty. Why could she see a path forward for Justine, but only walled-off corridors for herself?

Angel rested her palms on the cool faux-marble countertop and studied her reflection in the mirror. She looked calm and confident, celery-green face mask and bunny ears and all. *We're going to make some changes around here. Got that?* Then her phone pinged with a message and she tabled the pep talk.

BEST MALE LEAD: I'm here. Just parked.

Angel was in her bra and panties. She grabbed a towel off the rack, wrapped it around her chest and raced out of the apartment. Her heart thundered; she so badly wanted to see him. From the breezeway corridor, she had a view of the parking lot. She searched for the flashy little sports car and, not finding it, noticed the man dismounting a motorcycle. She would have recognized that walk anywhere.

There was her lover...

Angel had her phone with her and she called him. His phone lit up and he raised it to his ear. "Hey!" she said, teasing. "Look at you, easy rider!"

He looked up and spotted her. "No... Look at *you*, little bunny."

She laughed and brought a hand to her bunny ears. "I gave up on you. I was going to take a bath."

His golden voice filled her ears. "That sounds good. May I join you?"

"It's not a big Jacuzzi tub like you're used to."

"You have no idea what I'm used to."

"That's true."

"I stopped by *Diablo* and grabbed your favorites. After a bath we can get dirty and eat with our fingers."

That sounded delicious. "Come on up! The door's unlocked."

Angel rushed back into her bathroom to wash the green paste off her face and gurgle with mouthwash, just in case. She came out to find him in the kitchen, unpacking the bags of takeout and sliding the containers into the refrigerator. He looked at ease in her home and familiar with her kitchen setup. It made her heart smile. How had it been only a week? She had lived in this apartment with Chris for months and it had never felt this good.

Alessandro, though, did not look good. His striking face was marked with fatigue and his bronze complexion had gone ashen. She'd nearly forgotten their day had begun with such fantastic news. They should have gone out to dinner with his friends. They should have celebrated with champagne. Instead, his day had been jam-packed with unpleasant tasks: speeding her back to the mainland, waiting around while she endured an FBI interrogation, learning from Justine that his beloved niece had betrayed him, then having to confront this niece. That was a lot to pack into twenty-four hours.

She went to him and touched his face. "How did it go?"

He took her hand and brought it to his lips. "I don't want to talk about it."

"Understood."

He slid the last container into the refrigerator and swung the door shut with more force than necessary. "No... I want to talk about it."

"Okay." Angel folded her arms across her chest, mainly to hold her towel in place. "I'm listening."

"She did it for the money."

That much Angel had figured out. But as far as get-rich-quick schemes went, this one was pretty elaborate. There had to be easier ways to make fast cash. However, her professional curiosity prevailed. "Who forged your grandfather's work?"

"She did."

His beloved niece was a mastermind forger, too? "Are you sure? That takes skill."

His broad shoulders drooped. "She's a talented artist."

"I don't get it. Why not just sell her own art then?"

"I asked the same question," he replied wearily. "She's not interested in building a career over years and years and years. She wanted fast cash."

Angel winced. That description, minus the criminal element, was how she'd describe herself. She wasn't interested in building a career over years. She'd given up because the struggling artist phase had dragged on for too long and too many people were waiting in the wings for her to fail. Alessandro, who hadn't given up or sought fast cash, who'd worked as a bartender, waiter, janitor and who knows what to bankroll his dreams, was reaping the rewards.

"She's also a talented businesswoman," he said. "Buyers are willing to pay good money for a famous actor's grandfather's secret paintings. She leaked the story and the waitlist got longer."

Angel was overcome with sadness. It was terrible that his niece thought nothing about using him that way.

"The money was for my brother, Eddy. He's in trouble and risks losing his house and his business. The paintings didn't go for much. Fifty grand here. Forty grand there. It was enough to save my brother's house from foreclosure."

"Oh...wow..."

He looked down at his scuffed boots. "Yeah."

Angel waddled over and leaned heavily on him, even though her intention was to lend him support. "What are you going to do?"

"I'm going to give her the money."

"What? No!"

"Yes."

She jerked away "You're rewarding bad behavior! They could have just asked you for a loan, you know. Have you thought about that?"

"You'd think so, but my brother didn't want my dirty money."

Angel was confused. "Repping Rolex watches on the side isn't exactly shameful."

"The money is dirty because I'm dirty. I'm the kid of some woman my dad picked up at a bar during *Calle Ocho Festival*, and I'm not deserving of success."

Angel's skin prickled with revulsion. "She told you this to your face?"

He raised his hands to his head and interlaced his fingers. "I knew they thought that way, but honest to God, Angel…"

"Alessandro…" she whispered. "I'm so sorry. Your family—"

"I don't think I can call them my family, Angel," he said. "They're relatives, not family."

She did not know what to say to that. Rather than offer him empty words of consolation, she let the silence do its work. When the flash of pain had dimmed in his eyes, she took him by the hand. "Come," she said. "Let's get into that bath before it gets cold."

In the bathroom, Angel undressed him and dropped his clothes onto the vanity bench. He stepped into the tub with a splash. She eased in and got settled, her back to his chest. "Hope you like lavender."

"Love it." His hands moved all over her body, roaming everywhere.

Angel twisted around and sought his mouth. She kissed him again and again, deeper and deeper. In need of more, she swiveled onto her knees. Sudsy water splashed onto the pink floral tile. He yanked the headband off her head, tangled his fingers with her hair and pulled her to him. They kissed until it felt as if they were both sinking. Their wet bodies slipped and slid as water swirled around them. All she could hear was her own whimpering, the splash of water against tile, his drowned-out moans. Alessandro gripped her bottom and forced her still. "We have to get out," he said, breathing fast. "I want you now."

Angel kissed him once again before pushing away and rising to her feet. She extended a hand to Alessandro, but his gaze poured over her dripping wet body. When he looked at her like that, she felt beautiful, desirable and bold.

His eyes trailed after her as she stepped out of the tub.

The bathmat was soaking wet under her feet. The cold air streaming through the A/C vent hardened her nipples. Angel met his gaze and did not reach for a towel. "When you collect yourself, you'll know where to find me."

Twenty-Three

"Let's eat!" she said.

Angel had set up a buffet on the coffee table. Sandro dropped down on the couch. He'd worked up a healthy appetite, but her greedy grin made him want to propose they do something else entirely. After all, they'd made good use of this couch before. He knew if he tried anything, Angel would stab him with a fork.

She opened a cardboard container and gasped. "The mac and cheese! My favorite!"

Her delight was pure. Grabbing dinner at *Diablo* had been a smart move. It would make what he had to do next so much easier. Maybe.

"Angel, I have to leave in the morning."

"Back to paradise," she teased, and handed him the carton of spicy meatballs.

"Back to work."

His publicist had called again. FastFlix wanted him

available for promotional work and Cameron demanded he make up lost ground from the "epic Emmys snub." *We need you out there, reminding the people why they love you.* Any award could potentially be the last. He had to make the most of it. The nomination could raise his profile, his clout, his pay grade and anything else he could possibly raise.

Angel was sitting very still, her fork loaded with mac and cheese suspended halfway between the paper plate on her lap and her lips. She'd piled her wavy hair on the top of her head and held the unruly mass together with a pair of clips. This left her long, slender neck exposed. But if he leaned over to kiss that spot below her ear, she would stab him for real this time.

"I promised you more time…" Angel would not look at him. He pressed on. "The award nomination changes everything. I have to do a lot of press."

"The Golden Globes," she mused. "An amazing opportunity."

Sandro hesitated before taking the plunge. "Would you come with me?"

She set her plate on the coffee table as if the food were poisonous. "Where to?"

He presented his itinerary as if it were the adventure of a lifetime. "Up the coast to New York City, then cross country to LA."

"No."

Her blunt answer wounded him.

"I'm not asking you to move in with me," he said defensively. "Only to hang out a while. We can spend the holidays together."

"My dad is celebrating his sixtieth birthday this Christmas," she said. "Plus I have things to do here."

"What things? The gallery is closed," he reminded her.

"And they can lose my number," she said. "I will never work for them again."

"What then? Orlando?" Did she want to go home? Was that it?

"No," she said. "I'll stay here and sort myself out."

Sandro had lost his appetite. So long, spicy meatballs. "Angel, you don't have to have your life all figured out. Not for my sake, anyway."

"Actually, I do." Her voice was a tortured whisper.

He'd wanted to protest, but the words died in his mouth. Who was he to lecture her? He'd avoided serious relationships all through his twenties for those same reasons. He'd wanted his career on track. It had taken a few hit movies and a variety of awards to get him to slow down enough to allow a woman like Angel into his life.

"This is a good thing," she said. "Do the press, the Globes, film your movie, all of it. Next time you're in town, we'll hang out."

She hadn't yet finished her thought and Sandro was shaking his head. "How about you come up with another plan."

She crossed her legs. Her silky robe parted to reveal a flash of smooth brown thigh. Again he struggled to keep his hands to himself. As much as he wanted to touch her, he had to listen. This was important.

"I've been thinking about this. We are no way near what you're proposing."

Sandro grabbed a napkin to wipe his mouth, but really just to do something with his hands. She'd been thinking about them spending time apart? This was news to him.

"Will you fly out for the awards?" he asked. "You're my date."

"No." She held her ground. "That's something a couple in a committed relationship would do, don't you think?"

If she needed him to commit, he'd commit, no problem. "Angel, I—"

She grabbed his arm as if to prevent him from saying something rash. "None of this was supposed to matter. Remember? You were always meant to leave, and I was always meant to get on with my life."

Sandro got up to get a beer from the refrigerator. He needed to cool down. He found the bottle opener in the utensil draw and snapped off the cap of the *Corona Light*, the only beer she kept in stock. A strange feeling moved through him. He felt more at home at her rental apartment than at Fisher Island or LA. This was a feeling that had eluded him for years. He hadn't had a home since JD's death.

He abandoned the beer bottle on the countertop and went to her. Hunching low before her, he anxiously slid his hands to her waist. He could lose her if he didn't handle this right. *"Querida—"*

"NO!" Angel smashed his face between her hands to silence him. "No Spanish! That's not fair!"

He peeled her hands away and kissed them. "Sorry. Didn't know it had that kind of effect on you." He made his feelings known in plain old English. "I don't want to lose you."

Her eyes glazed with tears. "I don't want you to lose me, either. I'm phenomenal."

"Yes, you are."

"And so are you, but I can't dream with you anymore, Alessandro. I've woken up to the truth."

"Angel... I know I hurt you and broke my promise."

We tell each other the things that matter.

He'd had no business making such a promise, unfairly earning her trust, at a time when he was withholding so much from her.

"It doesn't matter any more."

"You're giving up?"

"I told you: we orbit around different suns."

"That doesn't mean anything!"

He could tell by the tilt of her head that there was nothing he could say to reach her.

"Trust me," she said. "It's better this way."

Sandro brushed his lips to hers, wishing to God he could take away the pain he'd caused. When he pulled back, the taste of her tears was on his tongue. He didn't say it, but he committed to her right then and there.

The next morning, they woke up at six, as per her routine. Only this time Sandro didn't protest. It was all arranged. He was flying out to New York City this evening to report at the NBC studios tomorrow at dawn. She agreed that it was better for him to leave before rush hour traffic made moving around the city difficult. He had to return Gus's bike and stop by the restaurant to speak with Myles.

Angel had made coffee and they talked quietly for a while. Then she walked him to the parking lot. The day was fresh. Neighbors on their way to work cast curious glances their way as they drove by, maybe finally recognizing the Hollywood actor that had been coming in and out of their apartment complex. Sandro was oblivious to all that. The breeze played with the palm trees that lined the asphalt lot. Little green lizards darted between the low-cut shrubs. The sprinklers stuttered and sprayed cool water. He hugged Angel tight and breathed in the familiar scent of her skin. He hadn't shaved. She rubbed her cheek against his stubble.

"Can we keep in touch?" he asked sheepishly.

"We can," she said. "Nothing forced though. Whatever feels good."

Sandro groaned. He hated her noncommittal tone.

She tilted her head back and searched his face. "You're going to be on a movie set for months. Have fun!"

"Fun?" he said. "It's work. What do you think I'm going to do? Hook up with extras in my trailer?"

"If you're going to hook up with anybody," she said, "at the very least, make it your costar."

"It's a fantasy thriller. My costars are a robot and a green screen."

"Some of those robots are really sexy!"

"Will they laugh and cry at the same time, though?"

She laughed and brushed back a tear. "Go!" she said. "Go and be amazing."

"What are you going to do?"

"I'm going to be smart for a change."

"Will you remember me, your dumb mistake?"

She gave him a smile as fresh as the day. "Always."

Myles greeted him with a bear hug. "Mr. Golden Globes!"

Sandro had parked in the alley behind the restaurant and found Myles at the back door receiving a delivery of vegetables.

"I'm heading back to LA," Sandro said.

"How long this time?"

"I'll be lucky if I get back before the spring. After the awards, I'm taking off to film in New Zealand."

"Damn." The kitchen smelled like coffee. Myles poured him a cup. "I just got used to you coming around, disrupting my morning routine."

Sandro took his coffee to his usual seat at the prep counter. "I thought you liked peace and quiet."

"Nobody likes that much peace and quiet."

Myles heated up his favorite chocolate pastry and set it before him. "You don't even have to beg this time."

"Thanks, man." Sandro stirred sugar into his coffee and stared blindly into the cup.

"You okay?" Myles asked.

"I'm not okay," Sandro admitted. "Angel is through with me. I've lost her."

Sandro pushed back his coffee cup, breaking into a cold sweat. He'd lost his angel and had no one to blame but himself. He could not have messed up more spectacularly if he'd planned it.

"I don't buy it," Myles said. "Anyway, you two were fast and furious. Maybe it's a good idea to pump the brakes a little, slow it down."

Gigi had said something similar, except she'd used the words *hot and heavy*. She'd managed to spin Angel's refusal to accompany him to the Golden Globes as a positive. "That's a good thing! I'd be far more concerned if she wanted to jump into the limelight with you."

"That means you'll have to jump into the limelight," he said. "I need a date. Please don't make me go with my publicist."

"You can count on me!" Gigi said. "Jumping into the limelight is my favorite sport."

Now Myles was looking at him with a goofy expression. Sandro lost his cool. "She said we orbit around different suns."

"What does that mean?"

"I have no idea!"

"Astrology maybe?"

Sandro glared at Myles.

"Eat your *pain chocolat*," Myles said. "You'll feel better."

Sandro chomped down half of the pastry with one big

bite. While he chewed, he observed his childhood friend. He looked okay, but he always looked okay. Something was off. "What's going on with you?"

Myles shrugged. "Same old."

"Don't give me that," Sandro said. "I come here all the time and complain my ass off. The least you can do is give me something. Family, sex life, the restaurant..." Myles shifted slightly, but Sandro caught it. "The restaurant! Bingo!"

Myles circled the empty kitchen. Soon his prep staff would arrive and he would clam up. Sandro cut to the chase. "I risk losing man points by saying this, but here goes. I love you."

"Yo, man points are dead currency," Myles said.

"I'm being sincere," Sandro said. "I want us to grow old together, meet twice a week on a park bench and catch up while our grandkids run around."

Sandro had lost his family on this trip. Maybe his relationship with Sabina could be salvaged. Maybe not. She was not the person he thought she was. They'd have to get reacquainted and start over from zero. He would leave it up to her. His relationships with his friends were a different story. Sandro was prepared to fight to preserve them.

Myles tossed a balled-up dishtowel, aimed at Sandro's head. "What grandkids? I'm not having any kids, let alone grandkids."

"Your granddogs then."

"That's cool."

"What's going on with this place? It's packed every night."

"It's not my place, though, is it?" Myles said. "I put everything I have into it, but it's not mine. I hear the owners are thinking of selling."

Ah... *Diablo* was just one of the many restaurants

owned by a faceless conglomerate. Restaurants were risky business. Even rich people weren't rich enough to carry the losses. But Myles had proven that he was bankable.

Sandro had an idea, but first he got Myles up to speed on the Sabina affair. "My niece forged the paintings."

Myles's eyes widened. "No shit?"

"Absolutely none," Sandro said, resigned.

His friend took the wooden stool beside him. "What's the plan?"

"The plan is to shake down my agent and have her line up some endorsement deals. Cars, cologne, Fabergé eggs, I don't care."

"Hey! You have to care!" Myles protested. "You've got a brand to protect."

Sandro waved off his concerns. "Part of that money is going to save my brother's sorry business. And the rest, I could invest in another venture."

Myles face went taut. "I can't take your money."

No one wanted to take his money and frankly he was sick of it. "If you want your own place, you need to raise capital," he said. "Would you rather Sabina whip up a few paintings for you to sell?"

Sandro could hardly finish the sentence, he was laughing so hard. Myles slapped him on the back. "You are one sick dude!"

He had to laugh, even as he pressed the heels of his hands over his eyes to keep from crying. In the past few days, he'd experienced every emotion known to man. It was enough to crack a man in two.

Suddenly, Myles pulled him into a hug that felt like a chokehold. "You're a good friend and a great guy. Something tells me Angeline knows this and you don't have anything to worry about."

Twenty-Four

Alessandro was gone. As Angel watched him speed away on the borrowed bike, panic surged inside her. Unsure that she'd done the right thing, she tried to imagine an alternate ending. None came to mind. She and Alessandro had rushed into something they were not prepared for. Attraction was there, intimacy and friendship, too, but fundamental trust was not.

Back in her apartment, Angel crawled into bed and slept for hours. Her sheets smelled like him and, as the day dragged on, she was reluctant to leave her bed. He'd called on his way to the airport. Although he was up for an acting award, Angel delivered a stellar performance. She chatted happily and sounded upbeat when she wished him a safe trip.

In the evening, she ate their leftovers straight out of the cartons. Call it a miracle, but the creamy, buttery mac and cheese revived her. Bottom line: she would see him again.

At some point, he'd return to Miami. When that day came, she did not want to be the woman he'd left behind. She would use this time to change her life.

Angel took a container of roasted brussels sprouts to her computer desk and fired up Google. *Okay! Let's see what's out there for me.*

The first package arrived on Friday. The delivery guy knocked on her door and left the stiff envelope on her doormat. Running late for a job interview, she picked it up and tossed it onto the kitchen table. Later that night, while eating supermarket sushi, she noticed the envelope sitting on top of the stack of mail. She opened it, her fingers sticky with soy sauce. Inside was a single sheet of paper. She slid it out and blinked in disbelief. It was a simple ink sketch of a woman.

Angel grabbed a napkin and wiped her hands. Then with the tip of a finger, she traced the wavy hair, wide-set eyes, long nose, and full lips curled into a faint, enigmatic smile. The drawing was not signed. She checked the envelope again. The sender was "AC Enterprises." After a good laugh, she snapped a photo of the drawing and sent it to Alessandro. He called her right away. On impulse, she answered, forgetting the days of gut-wrenching silence that had followed his departure.

"Hello," she said. "Is this the CEO of AC Enterprises?"

"Speaking."

"You drew this?"

"Sabina didn't get all the talent. I can handle a pen."

"You can handle more than a pen."

"The pen is mightier than whatever you have in mind."

Angel laughed. "I love it so much!"

"I drew it that first morning, after I spotted you running along the dock to catch the ferry. Good times."

"I was so scared that morning," she said in her defense. "The whole experience was too intense."

"Are you still scared?"

"Yes!" she said.

"I've missed you."

There was no way she could express how deeply and desperately she had missed him. She said goodbye and ended the call.

Every Friday after that, an envelope arrived. Each contained a new sketch that pulled her back to the time they had spent together. He drew her laughing, sleeping, reading and sipping a cup of coffee. If she were critiquing this work, she would have noted the obvious pandering to the male gaze. However, in this case, she didn't seem to mind.

She didn't mind when he started calling more regularly, at the start of his day. While he poured his first cup of coffee, Angel was on her second cup. He'd send her selfies at all hours and gave her virtual tours of the green rooms of every major show he'd booked. When bedtime came around, at least on her coast, they'd text until she fell asleep.

One night, she decided to tease him.

BEST MALE LEAD: So what are you up to?

ANGEL'S PHONE: I'm peeling off my T-shirt because I'm so hot...

Her phone rang immediately. "As much as I love where you're going with this, I want to know what you're up to regarding work."

"Oh." She sat fully dressed on the edge of her bed.

"I haven't pressed you on this because I know you need space," he said.

"Uh-huh." She hadn't brought up work because there was nothing to bring up. She'd gone through a round of interviews and was waiting to hear back.

"Angel, you can talk to me," he said. "I'm not going to judge you. Remember those early years when I was working as a—"

"Bartender/waiter/janitor," she chanted. "Yes, I know."

"Yeah, well," he said. "Going months between acting jobs was tough and humiliating. If I didn't have friends to talk to I would've gone crazy."

Angel knew exactly how he'd felt. She was already dreading the holidays in Orlando.

"I have a few promising leads," she said weakly.

"Let's hear it."

She told him about her interviews for positions at two prominent art museums. These were entry-level positions and would not pay much. But either one would go a long way to erasing the stain of Gallery Six on her résumé.

"Okay." His voice held no trace of enthusiasm.

"One of those museums is the Pérez," she said. "I'd be lucky to get a job there."

"Maybe..." he said. "What would you really want to do, given the chance?" Angel closed her eyes, weary, while he continued. "What about your own art? Why haven't I seen it yet?"

"You've seen my paintings."

"The few on your walls? Weren't you a kid when you painted those?"

"Well...yes."

"Plus they're paintings of a country you've never visited."

"What does it matter? I will someday."

"And I'll visit Cuba someday. Maybe we'll go on a pilgrimage together. My point is: I know what it's like to be haunted by a lost homeland."

More than anything, Angel loved how much they had in common. Their respective family trees had been violently uprooted from the Caribbean and planted on Florida shores without the benefit of a soil study or even fertilizer. As a result, they were hybrid individuals bearing all sorts of odd fruit. But that was where the similarity ended. Alessandro had the freedom to experiment. Angel was trapped in a box. In a desperate attempt to earn her parents' approval, she had limited herself to producing the kind of art they admired and collected. And now she was stuck with the artist's version of writer's block.

"As they say in LA, pretty angel, bloom where you're planted."

She hated to break it to him, but they said that everywhere, though mainly online. "Are you suggesting that I paint Lincoln Road Mall?"

"Or just the view outside your window," he said. "Why not? We're here now. Florida is home."

"Technically, you're in California."

"But where is my heart?"

Angel spilled onto her back and drew her knees to her chest. *Oh, be still, stupid heart!*

Angel knew what Alessandro was doing with his sketches, texts, photos and phone calls and it was working. A few days ago, he'd asked in a soft voice whether she could ever forgive him. She'd said yes. Even so, she wasn't prepared to toss caution in the wind and start up with him again.

"Hey, it's late," he said. "I'll let you get some sleep."

"What if I try again and it doesn't work?" she blurted.

Her question had two layers. The pause before his answer told her that he understood.

"What if it does?"

"Okay, but what if it doesn't?"

"Well then you'd have tried. No regrets."

After they'd said goodnight, Angel tapped on the digital drawing app on her phone and scrolled through her portfolio. She considered sharing her sketches with Alessandro, but compared to her oil paintings, all neatly packed away at her parents' house, these seemed so basic. Would he laugh?

Her gaze drifted to her bedroom walls, which she'd turned into a gallery showcasing the drawings delivered to her door every Friday. Each quick sketch was precious to her. She would never judge them or laugh at his technique. They brought her so much happiness and sparked pinwheels of joy.

Before Angel lost her nerve, she selected a few of her digital sketches and forwarded them along.

Her phone rang immediately.

THE RED CARPET STYLE EVOLUTION OF HOLLYWOOD'S LEADING MAN

Alessandro Cardenas is nominated for acting in a supporting role; nevertheless, he remains our leading man. The Cuban American actor caused a stir the moment he stepped onto his first red carpet in Armani Privé. He has been turning heads ever since. Here are some of our favorite looks. (Click for slideshow)
—@Vanities_Fashion_IG

Twenty-Five

No sketch arrived on the Friday before the Golden Globes. Angel assumed that Alessandro was busy with fittings, press junkets, dinners and after-parties. On Saturday morning, he called to say that he'd be MIA through Sunday. "It's a crazy circus."

"I understand. And I'm rooting for you."

She had rented *Black Market*. His performance as a disillusioned cop had been flawless.

"Thanks, Angel," he said. "Love you."

Her belly tightened. "Love you, too."

Love you was the kind of thing you said to a friend and she refused to read too much into it. Plus, Angel had her own schedule to stick to. She had resumed waking up at six to paint, except this time she left her apartment with only an iPad and a stylus. Her new project was an expansion of her lunch break excursions, only now she ventured past Lincoln Road to Little Haiti, Little Havana, Wynwood and

Midtown. She picked a street and drew her surroundings, rendering the buildings and the people as she saw them. The drawings were vivid in a way still life paintings of fruit could never be. In no time, she had developed quite a portfolio. Digital art was a dynamic field. There were no shortage of grants and residencies. Angel applied for a few. She was particularly excited about a residency at a prestigious institute. She could not bring herself to hope and told no one, not even Alessandro, out of fear of jinxing it.

Angel spent Saturday in Coral Gables, sketching a stretch of Ponce de Leon Boulevard. But she could not stop thinking of Alessandro. Did he have a pre-award show ritual? Did it consist of a standard massage, shave and haircut, or was it more elaborate? She imagined him holed up in a Beverly Hills hotel with a team of professionals fussing over him. As his date, would she have received one of those famous goodie bags chock-full of designer items—or was that reserved for the Oscars? Finally, why had she passed on the opportunity to attend an awards show? Likely a once in a lifetime opportunity. By the end of the evening, she could have been hanging out with Tracee Ellis Ross and exchanging contact information with Amal Clooney. *You don't think, Angel. You just feel and react.*

That night, Angel fell asleep with her phone clutched in her hand. At two in the morning, she startled awake and found that she'd missed a text message.

BEST MALE LEAD: You don't know how much I miss you.

On Sunday Angel couldn't hold back. She called him. It was the morning of the Golden Globes and she wanted to hear his voice. She wanted to feel connected with him in some way. And she wanted to wish him luck one last time. She hoped he'd win.

The call went to voice mail.

Angel made breakfast and spent the morning searching the internet for scraps of information. Nothing! Most of the stories focused on what the actors would be wearing to the show, as if anyone cared. Why weren't the tabloids doing their job?

She was drizzling honey in her oatmeal when an email alert popped on her screen. She'd received a message from Art Tech, a resident artists program in Los Angeles. *Oh, God!* She crossed the room and plopped onto her couch. Finally! This was the message that she'd been waiting for, but to receive it on a Sunday... This couldn't be good. Maybe this was the gentle, letting-you-down softly email. The thanks, but no thanks message. There was no way to know until she read it.

Angel reached for a throw pillow and clutched it to her belly for support. What had started as a pipe dream had blossomed into so much more. She wanted this, or something similar. She wanted the opportunity to focus on her art, hone her voice and explore a new medium. If this turned out to be a politely worded rejection, she would howl with disappointment. For a moment, she fought the urge to toss her phone out the window. Angel quickly snapped out of it. She could survive bad news. A little disappointment never killed anyone, but dreading bad news could give her a heart attack.

She held her breath and tapped on the message.

Congratulations! You have been selected for a one-year artist-in-residency program at ART TECH in Los Angeles, California.

Holy shit!

Angel buried her face in the pillow on her lap and screamed. She screamed until her throat ached. At long last, something for her!

I won! I won! I won!

Alessandro won, too. A giddy actress opened a gold envelope and read his name off a card. Angel popped open a bottle of champagne. The overflow spilled onto her pajamas. The camera caught Alessandro's stunned expression. He was seated next to beautiful Gigi Garcia. She drew him into a hug and kissed his cheek. Angel watched as he trotted up the wide steps to the stage. He looked incredibly handsome in a classic black tuxedo. And as happy as she was, as proud as she felt, she couldn't beat away a sour feeling. This had been a big day for both of them and they should have enjoyed it together.

Alessandro could be counted on to put on a show and give the viewers at home what they wanted. He kissed the trophy and held it high, earning more applause. When the cries died down, he spoke into the microphone.

"This award is dedicated to my grandfather, the painter Juan David Valero, who taught me to value my art."

Angel's pajama top was wet with champagne, her face was wet with tears and she was turning into a pile of mush on the floor. But Alessandro wasn't done.

"My angel, I love you and I'm coming home."

The camera panned away. The next thing she knew, Angel was watching a commercial for the new Buick. She raised the champagne bottle to her lips with a shaky hand and gulped down a third.

The 5:00 a.m. knock on her door sent Angel flying out of bed. She'd been in a champagne-induced coma. Was the banging on her door and the buzzing of her phone real or imagined? She tiptoed to her apartment door. Her vision was too blurry for her to see anything through the peephole. Another knock and she jumped back.

"I'll call the police!" she cried, unsure why exactly. For all she knew it could have been her elderly neighbor.

"Oh, Angel, don't do that."

That voice!

Angel fumbled with the lock and swung open the door. There stood her leading man, a little disheveled but still devastatingly handsome in his classic tux. "Sorry," he said, sheepish. "I couldn't stay away a day longer."

She threw herself at him, any trace of shame gone. "I love you! So much!"

"That's a relief!" Laughing, he lifted her off the floor and carried her inside the apartment. He took care to lock the door behind them. "I love you, too. But are you alright?"

She ran a hand through her messy hair. "I had a lot of champagne."

"Told you champagne was overrated. I never touch the stuff."

"Well, I was celebrating!"

"Without me?"

She pouted. "It wasn't the same."

"I bet."

He swooped her up and carried her into the bedroom. They flopped onto her bed, laughing. As he peeled off his jacket, he noticed the framed sketches on the wall. "This is why I love you!" he exclaimed. "Those sketches are not worth the price of IKEA frames."

Angel rested a hand on his cheek. "Those frames are from Michael's. The sketches are priceless to me. I was sad I didn't get one on Friday."

Alessandro rubbed his face into her palm. "Friday was crazy. New Zealand is postponed indefinitely. They've released me from my contract."

She scrambled onto her side. "Are you serious?"

"Yes, and it's fine. I'm glad to be done with it. My grandfather raised me to be an artist, not a hollow movie star. I need to pick my projects more wisely."

Angel was moved beyond words. "He would be so proud of you."

"Thanks." He took her hand and laced their fingers together. "I hope so."

"What are your plans?"

"I've got a meeting with Knight Films—they're local. Maybe I'll move back to Florida full-time. What do you think?"

Angel made a face. He interpreted it the wrong way. "Too fast?"

"No, it's not that. I'm leaving Florida."

"You are?"

"Sorry, yes. I got accepted to a one-year artist residency."

"You have?" Alessandro went ashen gray. "I'm happy for you. Where will you be?"

"Los Angeles."

"Wait." He rolled off the bed and stood before her. "Say that again."

"I'm moving to Los Angeles." She searched his face. A strange mix of emotions was displayed there. "Too fast?"

He held her face between his hands. "Not for us," he said, and kissed her slowly.

Never for us.

Epilogue

LIVESTREAM

"Hey, everyone! Last Sunday at the Globes I forgot to thank a few very important people in my life. Some I've called and thanked privately. But I have to give a big shout out to my agent, Leslie Chapman.

Leslie, you're my rock and I couldn't do any of this without you.

Guys, it's been a crazy few weeks. I'm going to follow my agent's advice and take some time off. Don't come looking! I'm with my Angel in paradise, and we're going dark. I'll check in when we're back in LA. Until then, be good and take care!

@Sandro_Official.

Comments turned off.

* * * * *

**WE HOPE YOU ENJOYED
THIS BOOK FROM**

⬦HARLEQUIN
DESIRE

*Luxury, scandal, desire—welcome to
the lives of the American elite.*

Be transported to the worlds of oil barons, family dynasties,
moguls and celebrities. Get ready for juicy plot twists,
delicious sensuality and intriguing scandal.

6 NEW BOOKS AVAILABLE EVERY MONTH!

HDHALO2021

#2815 TRAPPED WITH THE TEXAN
Texas Cattleman's Club: Heir Apparent • by Joanne Rock
To start her own horse rescue, Valencia Donovan needs the help of wealthy rancher Lorenzo Cortez-Williams. It's all business between them despite how handsome he is. But when they're forced to take shelter together during a tornado, there's no escaping the heat between them...

#2816 GOOD TWIN GONE COUNTRY
Dynasties: Beaumont Bay • by Jessica Lemmon
Straitlaced Hallie Banks is nothing like her superstar twin sister, Hannah. But she wants to break out of her shell. Country bad boy Gavin Sutherland is the one who can teach her how. But will one hot night turn into more than fun and games?

#2817 HOMECOMING HEARTBREAKER
Moonlight Ridge • by Joss Wood
Mack Holloway hasn't been home in years. Now he's back at his family's luxury resort to help out—and face the woman he left behind. Molly Haskell hasn't forgiven him, but they'll soon discover the line between hate and passion is very thin...

#2818 WHO'S THE BOSS NOW?
Titans of Tech • by Susannah Erwin
When tech tycoon Evan Fletcher finds Marguerite Delacroix breaking into his newly purchased winery, he doesn't turn her in—he offers her a job. As hard as they try to keep things professional, their chemistry is undeniable...until secrets about the winery change everything!

#2819 ONE MORE SECOND CHANCE
Blackwells of New York • by Nicki Night
A tropical destination wedding finds exes Carter Blackwell and maid of honor Phoenix Jones paired during the festivities. The charged tension between them soon turns romantic, but will the problems of their past get in the way of a second chance at forever?

#2820 PROMISES FROM A PLAYBOY
Switched! • by Andrea Laurence
After a plane crash on a secluded island leaves Finn Steele with amnesia, local resident Willow Bates gives him shelter. Sparks fly as they're secluded together, but will their connection be enough to weather the revelations of his wealthy playboy past?

YOU CAN FIND MORE INFORMATION ON UPCOMING HARLEQUIN TITLES, FREE EXCERPTS AND MORE AT HARLEQUIN.COM.

HDCNM0721

"Listen." Carter broke the silence when they reached her door. "I didn't mean to upset you."

Phoenix cut him off. "Don't worry about it."

"I thought the timing was right. We were getting along and…"

"It's evident you still have an issue with timing," Phoenix snapped.

Her comment stung. Carter took a deep breath and exhaled slowly. He tried not to lose his patience with her.

"I'm sorry. I shouldn't have said that." Phoenix carefully stepped over the threshold and turned back toward Carter.

"I'm sorry, too. Hopefully we can move on. It was nice being friendly. Maybe one day we could go back to that."

Phoenix looked away. When she looked back at Carter, there was something unreadable in her eyes. Had she been more affected by his news than he realized? Their eyes locked. Carter felt himself moving closer to her.

"We just need to get through the wedding tomorrow and the next few days, and we can go back to living our normal lives.

You won't have to see me and I won't have to see you."

Phoenix's words struck something in him. He didn't like the idea of never seeing her again. The past few days had awakened something in him. Even the tense moments reminded him of what he once loved about her. He remembered his own words... *The way I love you.*

Carter kept his eyes on hers. She held his gaze. Old feelings returned, stirring his emotions. Perhaps those feelings had never left and remained dormant in his soul. His heart quickened. Desire flooded him and he wondered what Phoenix would do if he kissed her. She still hadn't looked away. Was she waiting for him to leave? Did she want to kiss him as much as he wanted to kiss her? Maybe she was having some of the same wild thoughts. Maybe old feelings were coming to the surface for her, too.

Carter stepped closer to Phoenix. She didn't move. Carter noticed the rise and fall of her chest become more intense. He stepped closer. She stayed put. He watched her throat shift as she swallowed. He smelled the sweet scent of perfume. He wondered if he could taste the salt on her skin.

Carter wasn't sure if it was love, but he felt something. It was more than lust. He missed Phoenix. The thought of her absence burned in him. In this moment he realized every woman since her had been an attempted replacement. That's why none of those relationships worked. But Phoenix would never have him. Would she?

Don't miss what happens next in...
One More Second Chance *by Nicki Night.*

Available August 2021 wherever
Harlequin Desire books and ebooks are sold.

Harlequin.com

Iris Daniels wondered if there was a particular art to changing your life. If so, then she wanted to find it. If so, she needed to. Because she'd about had enough of her quiet baking-and-knitting existence.

Not that she'd had enough of baking and knitting. She loved both things.

Like she loved her family.

But over the last couple of months, she had been turning over a plan to reorder her life.

It had all started when her younger sister, Rose, had tried to set her up with a man who was the human equivalent of a bowl of oatmeal.

Iris didn't like to be mean, but it was the truth.

Iris, who had never gone on a date in her life, had been swept along in her younger sister's matchmaking scheme. The only problem? Elliott hadn't liked her at all.

Elliott had liked Rose.

And Iris didn't know what bothered her more. That her sister had only been able to imagine her with a man when he was so singularly beige, or that Iris had allowed herself to get swept along with it in the first place.

Not only get swept along with it, but get to the point where she had convinced herself that it was a good thing. That she should perhaps make a real effort to get this guy to like her because no one else ever had.

That maybe Elliott, who liked to talk about water filtration like some people talked about sports, their children or once-in-a-lifetime vacations, was the grandest adventure she would ever go on.

That she had somehow imagined that for her, dating a man who didn't produce any sort of spark in her at all, simply because he was there, was adventure.

That she had been almost eager to take any attention she could, the idea of belonging to someone, feeling special, was so intoxicating she had ignored reality, ignored so many things, to try to spin a web of lies to make herself feel better.

That had been some kind of rock bottom. Truly terrifying.

It was one thing to let yourself get swept away in a tide of years that passed without you noticing, as things around you changed and you were there, inevitably the same.

It was quite another to be complicit in your own underwhelming life. To have willingly decided to be grateful for something she hadn't even wanted.

Don't miss
The Heartbreaker of Echo Pass
by New York Times *bestselling author Maisey Yates, available July 2021 wherever Harlequin books and ebooks are sold.*

HQNBooks.com